To: Nurse Vicky
U love you much!
Thanks,
Aisha

Other Titles by Aisha Johnson :

"I Am" a poetry collection

When Two Come Together

When Two Come Together

A Novella
by

Aisha Johnson

Nubiangodess Publishing
Columbus, Georgia

Copyright © 2003 by Aisha Johnson
ISBN 0-9744291-6-3

Cover Graphic by Angela Weathered
Book Formating by Kurt Weathered

All rights reserved. No part of this publication may be reproduced, stored in a retrieval system, or transmitted in any form or by any means, electronic, mechanical, recording or otherwise, without the prior written permission of this publisher, except in the case of brief quotations embodied in critical articles or reviews.

This is a work of fiction. It is not meant to depict, portray, or represent any particular organization or group of people. Names, characters, places, and incidents are the products of the author's imagination or are used fictitiously. Any resemblance to actual events, locales, or persons, living or dead, is entirely coincidental.

Published in the United States of America by Nubiangodess Publishing, Columbus, Georgia.

Acknowledgements

I can't believe I am at this portion of the process again! I would like to first thank the Creator for my gift and my passion. After giving this writing gig some serious thought I decided to add a mission statement along with my work. That mission statement is to enlighten, entertain, and/or educate my people through written expression. The purpose of " When two come together" is to enlighten as well as to entertain. This novel is a reflection of what it is really like when two people come together. First of all, there is always drama. Secondly, we are not perfect. However, love really does conquer all. I would like to thank my mother for continuing to believe in me. I don't know how she just does it. She is an amazing person. That is why I am dedicating this book to her and my dad. Daddy, I love you so much. Thanks to Doriyan, Antjuan, Bri'unna, Kesha, Tameka, Monquelle, Martise, Marsha, Monica, Alanah, Shenay, Alex, and Carlos. Thanks to my other momma's, Ms. Vicky, Ms. Yvas, Ms. Janette and Ms. Hederson. To the staff of Brown Diva Jazz, Janellle, Raynata, Anna and Alania, you diva's are the best. A special thank you to Angela and Kurt . There are no words for your hard work, patience, and commitment, only tears. (I am crying again). Good luck and much support to the Nubiangodess Publishing family Kim, Evelyn, Ms. Sammie, and Wanda. To my faithful fans, One love, Thanks for receiving my words.

Aisha

P.S. Please be sure to pre-order of you copy of "His Infidelities," it is too hot...

When Two Come Together

Prologue

The City of Dreams

Simone looked around her bedroom, for a quick second it didn't seem so small anymore. A single tear fell from her face. She didn't understand what she was feeling. On one hand, she was living out her dream and she was overjoyed. On the other hand, She was leaving behind her grandmother, and although they were deceased, her parents. This made her feel uneasy. Simone had always dreamed of living in New York City. Although Simone loved her grandmother very much, she wanted to her own life. She had already landed a great job, and she wouldn't be alone, Jessica and Meka were coming too. This was their plan. It was too late to turn back now they had found an apartment and everything. She picked up a picture of her deceased parents an in a whisper she spoke to them. *I did it.* She placed the picture back down on her dresser. She walked slowly through her Grandmothers house, she was in such a daze that she couldn't hear all the noise her family making. She walked over to the bookshelf and pulled out the Big Blue Bible that her grandmother had read to her as a child and opened up and began reading. She needed to come to peace with leaving her grandmother. Graham was a jazzy woman. She was beautiful, smart and very loving. When Simone parents died, she got custody of Simone. Although her grandmother was not wealthy, she made due after the Social Security checks stopped coming. She introduced Simone to writing poetry and to the Bible. She raised Simone to be independent and strong-minded for that Simone knew she would love her grandmother forever. One thing was very clear, her grandmother did not want either of her grandchildren to move to New York City. She had said that a city like that would corrupt her babies.

" Simone-" Her Aunt called out to her

" Ma'am," Simone looked up with tears falling from her eyes.

" It is time to go." Her voice softened when she saw that her niece was crying. " Go tell your Grandmother bye." Simone closed the book and carried into her Grandmothers bedroom. She placed it on the bed next to where her grandmother was lying. She was crying to hard to speak. Her grandmother wrapped her arms around her. She could tell that her grandmother had been crying too.

"Are you still mad because I am leaving?" Simone managed asked.

" Nope," Her grandmother answered.

When Two Come Together

"Well, this is it unh? " Simone hesitated and handed over her door key.

"Simone you may live in New York, But this is home." Graham didn't accept the key." Call me when you get there."

"Yes, ma'am" Simone started to walk away.

"Did I do a good job raising you?" Graham questioned Simone.

"It only took God 7 days to create heaven and earth. Graham, I am 23." She replied.

" Good," Graham picked up the blue bible and started to read. Simone wiped her tears away, and headed to the living room.

"Where you been?" Jessica asked Simone.

"Saying bye to Graham, y'all ready" She looked around for Meka.

"We will be as soon as Meka, finish talking to Rod" Jessica pointed to the door.

"Rod, oh no," Simone giggled. "We are leaving it all behind." she walked out to the front porch where Meka was talking to her ex-boyfriend. "Hey Rod" Simone waived.

"Hey Simone" He smiled. " You ready for the big move?"

Simone stood so that her cousin could see facial expression. "I am ready to leave it all behind."

Meka looked up at her cousin and started to laugh. Simone walked back in the house to get her last bag and, within in minutes they were at the Birmingham, Airport.

The girls rode the plane in complete silence. Each on thinking about what New York had in store for them. Simone dream was pretty simple. She wanted to become a true New Yorker. She wanted the upscale apartment, the 9-5 job, and a Wall Street man to go with it. When they reached New York City, they could barely keep up. Things were moving so fast. They stood outside for 15 minutes just trying to hail a cab. They had no luck. Finally, a white man felt sorry for them and hailed them one. When they finally reached their apartment and got all the bags out of the cab, they were worn out and hungry. They decided to walk down to the Deli they saw blocks from their apartment.

They sat at a table near a window so they could see out into the city. The waitress came over to take their order." 4.50 for a ham sandwich," Meka complained." Hell naw."

"You knew the cost of living was high." Jessica whispered to her cousin.

"I ain't about to spend 5.00 on a sandwich, with no drink and chips." Meka crossed her arms. "I don't have no damn job, just interviews."

"I pay for it." Simone just wanted her to be quiet.

"In that case let me get two sandwiches, a bag of chips and a soda." The other girls ordered and they walked back to their apartment. Although

When Two Come Together

they sat on boxes and ate sandwiches they felt like the queens of New York.

The next morning Simone got up extra early. She caught a cab to the nearest grocery store. She wanted to cook her cousin's breakfast. As she walked out of the door a little black boy snatched her groceries out of her hand and took off running. So she had to go home empty handed.

"Are you alright," Jessica asked.

"Yea, I am fine." Simone pouted. "Just hungry as hell" They all laughed. The girls walked down to the Deli for breakfast and then to the grocery store. They unpacked everything and tried to make the apartment look like home. No matter what Simone did to her room, it still didn't look or feel like home. Frustrated she gave up. She went and stood on the balcony of the apartment looking out at the city of her dreams.

Simone found no justice the first day at work. It seemed that she was the only black face there. Besides receptionist and interns, she was the only woman. This made Simone feel uncomfortable. She was highly qualified for the position, she held and wasn't as if she was in their way. She was an photo editor. All she did was clean up the mess they made with the camera. Four men had asked her to get them coffee and she wasn't happy about that at all.

She didn't want to tell her cousins that the city of dreams had somehow became the city of nightmares. She hated her job, and she had been robbed. Maybe they picked the wrong city to live in. Simone looked out on the Balcony, She prayed to God to find strength to deal with the city. The next morning she marched into her job with a new found strength. When one of photographers asked her coffee Simone explained to him that she was neither a secretary nor an intern. It amazed her how from that day no one ever asked her make coffee again. As time passed Simone began to see that New York in a different light. She learned how to hail a cab. She was good at her job and the money started rolling in. She got her own apartment and even met a man.

When Two Come Together
Simone

Simone picked up the phone. She placed it down onto the base and braced herself. Hesitating she walked into the kitchen and grabbed a bottle of water and went back into the bedroom. She walked slowly over the table and picked up the phone "8-1-5," She called out as she dialed the exchange. Losing her nerve to complete the call she hung up the phone again. Simone sat on the edge of her bed and stared at the picture of the two of them together during happier times. It only frustrated her more. Before she could loose her courage she picked up the phone and dialed the number quickly 8-1-5-2-7-8-4. He answered.

"Hello," Mytchel spoke. Simone hesitated. She couldn't even speak to him. "Simone," he called out to her.

"Yea," Simone answered with an attitude.

"How are you?" He asked casually.

"Mytch cut the small talk," She snapped. " I need my purse."

"I'll bring it over later," Mytchel suggested.

"No! Drop it off at Meka's apartment." She demanded. He was the last person she ever wanted to see.

"I was thinking that maybe we could go out for lunch. That way we can spend some time together and talk about what happened the other day." He tried to reason with her.

"We ain't got shit to talk about!" She said coldly. A silence fell over the phone as Simone began to recall Friday night events in her head.

She and Mytchel were at his friend's engagement party. The people seemed really nice, and the food was good. Simone had found the perfect little black dress and her hair was flawless. Her most prized accessory was her beau, Mytchel DeWayne Alexander, a financial analyst.

They had been dating now for two years and were even talking about marriage. When one of Mytchel's old college buddies came over to the table for small talk, Simone excused herself. She thought that it would be the perfect time to check her hair and make-up. While renewing her lipstick in the restroom, she noticed a woman starring at her. Simone could tell by the lady's facial expression she was upset. If this woman's look could have killed, Simone would have dropped dead instantly.

"Hi" Simone spoke. Never looking back at the woman.

"So you are Simone Benson?" The woman asked walking closer to her, and folding her arms.

"Yes, and you are? Simone looked a little bit confused, as she looked at the woman through the mirror.

When Two Come Together

"I'm the woman whose husband you been sleeping with." The woman answered Simone with angry glare in her eyes.

Simone quickly whipped the smile off of her face.

"Oh, No you must have me confused with-" but before Simone could finish her statement the woman reached into her red bag and pulled out pictures. Simone turned around slowly to see the evidence. There were pictures of Mytchel and her together on what appeared to be their wedding day. There was even one with both of them and a little girl. Simone couldn't believe her eyes, it was the same little girl who Mytchel said was his niece.

"I- I don't" Simone hesitated. Before she could get the courage to look up at the woman, she was gone. Simone couldn't wrap her mind around the facts. She and Mytchel had spent countless nights together. *When did he even have time be that woman's husband?* She gathered her composure and went back to the party. When she got back over to the table Mytchel and his friend were still there talking. Each moment that the conversation went on seemed like eternity passing. Simone sat in her seat fighting her tears because she didn't want to cause a scene. When his friend finally walked away, Simone tried to calm herself.

"Mytch, there was this woman that - " Simone stopped and tried again. "Well, she came in the bathroom and-" Puddles of tears started to wail up in her eyes.

"Lisa is my wife." Mytchel explained to Simone nonchalantly.

Simone's head began to spin uncontrollably. The harder she tried to speak, the heavier her heart became. Simone was on verge of a break down. She barely managed to get up and out of there. She left her purse and keys on the table, but luckily for her, Ta Meka was home or she would not have even had the money to pay for the cab.

Simone broke the silence over the phone.

"Mytchel, I need my purse."

"I am on my way to bring it over" He responded.

"What makes you think that I would want to see you?" She snapped.

"You are a married man, Mytch. What other lies have you told?"

"I have never lied to you," He rebutted.

"You are lying now. I didn't know you had a wife and kids." Simone continued.

"It has been over between me and Lisa for years"

Mytchel tried to explain.

"Mytch, that is bull shit and you know it. Is that why you are still married to her?" Simone questioned.

"I am only with her for Morgan's sake." He tried to reason with her.

When Two Come Together

"Your niece?" Simone asked puzzled. " Look Mytch, you don't have to explain shit to me. You need to see a shrink. Nothing you can say or do will allow me to rationalize your sick reason for living a lie." Simone said coldly.

"She is my niece, let me explain what's been going on baby." He paused. "It is not what you think. I am at your door." Mytchel pleaded." Face to Face baby we can talk this out."

Simone ran to her mirror and fixed her hair. Not only did she feel like shit she looked like it too. " No Mytch ! Drop it off downstairs at Meka's or at Jessica's." she yelled. If she did decided to let him in, he wouldn't know that she had been crying since Friday night. She was heart broken but she still had her pride.

" Do you want to throw away two years? Don't you want to know why?" He filled her head with questions.

Simone walked into the living room. She did have a lot of questions. *Why did he have an apartment if he was married? Where had his wife been all of those nights when he spent the night with her?* Simone began to fluff the pillows in the living room. The phone was silent but she could hear him at the door.

"Baby, I love you." Mytchel continued to plead.

Simone opened the door. Mytchel walked in and threw her purse on the couch. She could tell he was nervous, because he still had the phone to his ear. She looked him over and noticed the wedding band on his finger. She moved closer to him and grabbed his hand and looked him in the face.

"Face to Face, Mytch, it is over." She motioned her finger as to say get out and slammed the door behind him.

Hot tears began to wail up in her eyes. She made her way back into her bedroom. She pulled the picture of the two them from her night stand and flung it across the room. Simone stared at the broken glass. To her, it was a reflection of the way her heart felt. She pulled out her Journal and began to write. As the words floated from her heart to the paper, she was usually able find peace of mind. Not tonight. Tonight, Simone would simply cry herself to sleep.

When Two Come Together

Jonathan

Jonathan ran over to the buzzer. Before he could push the button down the phone rang.
"Yea-" He yelled into the speaker
"Yo- this is Mark" The voice from the speaker called out. "Are you ready?"
"Come on up here dawg." He yelled back into the speaker. He sprinted to the phone.
"Hello" He answered, walking to unlock the door.
"Yo- this is Tony, Is Mark there yet?" Tony asked.
"Yea, He's here." Jonathan answered.
"Well I will be there in 15 minutes." Tony said. " We had a meeting that ran late at the office"
"It's on." Jonathan gave his approval and hung up the phone. He walked back into the living room and gave his boy a hand shake.
"Hey man," Jonathan said walking in to the next room. "What's up?"
"Nothing." Mark smiled.
"So how is the married life treating you?" Jonathan questioned.

"It's straight." Mark answered.

"Shannice got you on lock down," Jonathan joked.

"Man, whatever! How are you holding up?" Mark asked. "Are you dating again?"

"I've been out with a few freaks," Jonathan laughed he knew that would push Marks buttons. Mark was the sensitive one. He believed black women were queens. He couldn't stand for them to be treated like anything less.

"Baby boy, don't hurt yourself. All women aren't the same" Mark responded.

"I know that, I just haven't met the one for me yet." He smiled.

Jonathan walked into the bathroom and looked in the mirror. He was tired of people asking him about Tracey. He was definitely tired of seeing her face on almost every billboard in the city. It had been months since they split up. It wasn't like they were married or that she had died. They had simply broken up. She had gone too far this time. He couldn't forgive her for what she had done. She took a job in France without even consulting him first, pushed there wedding date back again, then she asked him if he would like to tag along. He supported her career locally, and thought the U.S., Hell even Canada, but not France. There was no way he'd be caught up in some woman's shadow. He was a successful software designer. Over the last four years women had practically thrown

When Two Come Together

themselves at him. He could have cheated; could have cheated plenty of times. Yet, he loved Tracey and would never do anything to hurt her. She was smart, beautiful and strong, just the way he liked his women. He just couldn't be tied down to someone who was never around. The buzzer rang again. It was Tony. The guys took off to Margarita night at Nikki's.

Aisha Johnson

Simone

Simone woke up to the sound of the door bell. She was almost certain it was one of her cousins, Jessica or Meka. She looked up and they were both there. They were always there for her when she needed them the most. They were her best friends and other than their grandmother they were all she had. Since Simone's parents had died in car crash when she was 8 years old, her grandmother and cousins became her family unit.

"How are you feeling?" Jessica asked stroking her cousin's uncombed hair.

"I am okay" Simone tried to smile.

"Good because we going to Nikki's tonight?" TaMeka grinned and snapped her fingers.

"NO-" Simone moaned. " I don't want to go to Nikki's." She whined.

"So, are you going to just sit at home and cry over that bum for the rest of your life?" Jessica teased

"Yes," Simone whined as she headed back into her bed. Jessica and Meka sat on opposite sides of her on the bed. They gave her the "there are more fish in the sea" talk and then Simone finally agreed to go to Nikki's. *At least there will be alcohol there,* she thought to herself. Within the

When Two Come Together

hour she was dressed and ready to go. Looking in the mirror at herself, she felt pretty again. Her cousins knew a trip to Nikki's was just what she needed to make her feel better.

Jonathan

The club's atmosphere was thick. Women there were all shapes, colors, and sizes. As the DJ played one of the hottest songs out, the people in the club dance butt to butt. Everyone seemed to be having a good time. It was hot and sweaty just the way a nightclub should be. The guys made their way to one of the few empty tables, and ordered their first round of Margarita's. While his boys made small talk, Jonathan looked around for his first victim.

"Tonya will be home in couple of months. Her agent is throwing her a big party," Tony said.

"Where at?" Mark asked.

"Some fancy ballroom," Tony said turning up his margarita.

"Well you know I am there." Jonathan stood up. " But for now, I have got to go and get with one of these lovely ladies sitting all alone" Jonathan finished his Margarita as fast as possible. He walked through the crowded club looking for a pretty girl. Once he spotted one he walked over and introduced himself. She was tall and slim in the waist. Her sun kissed brown face had no major flaws, so he took her on to the dance floor. She was even a good dancer. When he was ready for

When Two Come Together

round two he brought Shanna back over to the table and introduced her to his boys. During the course of the conversation, Shanna's dimples won Jonathan's attention for the rest if the night.

Aisha Johnson

Simone

When the girls stepped into the club it was already 11:00. It was crowed and extremely hot. As the ladies made their way through the club Meka spotted Mark. A guy from the accounting firm she worked at.

"Hey Mark" She flirted.

"Hey cutie," Mark grinned. "Have a seat," he offered pulling out a chair.

"I can't believe your wife let you out on a Sunday night," Meka giggled. " I thought your leash was on way tighter than that. " She joked. Meka introduced her cousins to Tony and Mark. Simone sat at the table in silence. She looked out at all of the people in the club smiling and dancing and decided those days were far behind her. She couldn't smile. She had lost the love of her life. She hadn't been in New York 2 weeks when she met Mytchel, and he was a direct reflection of what New York meant to her. He had gone practically everywhere with her except for Nikki's. He felt Nikki's was her spot to chill with her cousins. When she went to Nikki's on the occasional Sunday he would always stay at home. Once she left the club, she would go directly to his apartment where they would make love something serious and then the two of them would cook pancakes together. Simone's thoughts were interrupted by a tall, dark skinned man with long dreads.

"Excuse me," He greeted her. "Would you like to dance? "He extended his hand in a gentleman like fashion.

Simone looked around and decided she might as well.

"Sure, but I need a drink first," She answered. They walked through the crowded bar introducing themselves. Steven wasn't bad looking at all. He had the most beautiful eyes Simone had ever seen. Just as the bartender passed the margarita over to Simone, a guy elbowed her and made her waste her drink all over herself. Simone was furious. " I need to sit down" she said as she allowed Steven to wipe the drink off of her chest. Once they got back over to the table her cousin could see the anger in her eyes.

"What's the matter ?" Meka asked

"Some dude just made me spill my margarita all over my clothes," She complained.

"I can't see it" Jessica scanned the outfit a second time.

"He didn't even apologize," Simone continued.

"You still look pretty." Mark tried to make her feel better. "Maybe he didn't do it on purpose.

"Whatever!" Simone turned to get up as the guy who elbowed her walked up to the table.

"Who are these lovely ladies?" He smiled with excitement.

"Oh, he can speak." Simone stated sarcastically. "I thought he was an ape that escaped from zoo, but he can speak." Simone got up and started to walk a way. "I'm going home." Steven scurried behind her like a dog in heat. "Can I hail you a cab, pretty lady?" Steven offered.

"Nah, I feel like walking" Simone forced herself to smile.

"You know I can't let you walk the mean streets of New York alone. Can I walk with you?" he asked.

"Sure you can." Simone agreed. The two began to sing old show tunes and walk to Simone's Place. When they arrived at Simone's apartment building she could tell that Steven was impressed. Simone thought about going up to her cold, silent apartment and decided she didn't want to be alone." How about you come up to my apartment for a cup of tea?" She invited.

"It's getting late, so I can't stay for too long." He hesitated.

"Come on cutie" Simone flirted. She knew if he left she would only cry. She was tired of crying. " I don't bite." She grabbed his hand and led him up to her apartment. She poured the tea and put on a nice CD. " Before we talk, I need to have a shower." She said walking to the rear of the apartment. "Please don't leave." She yelled making her way down the hallway. Simone jumped in the shower.

The water felt so good against her skin. It seemed to cleanse her spirit and it made her feel beautiful again. She closed her eyes and envisioned Mytchel in the shower with her. She could almost feel him. Her thoughts were interrupted by the phone ringing. She quickly jumped out the shower and rushed into her bedroom to answer it.

"Hello" She answered.

"Hi, Simone," Mytchel called out casually.

"I have company." Simone slammed the phone down. As she made her way down the hall into the living room tears filled her eyes.

"Is everything okay?" Steven asked concerned.

"Yes, that was my ex-boyfriend" Simone tried to hold herself together.

"What happened?" Steven asked.

"He was a liar and cheater. He was also very much a part of my life." Simone couldn't hold it together any longer and tears began to fall. Steven reached for her and whipped her tears away. When he tried to kiss her she had no reservations. With every intention to comfort her Steven, used his soft lips to kiss her neck, her shoulders and then her breast. He took his time to give each nipple ample attention while he rubbed his middle finger along the edges of her vagina split in order to tease her. Simone could the jewel between her legs throbbing with excitement.

"Can I taste you?" He asked Simone's permission but he didn't wait for an answer. He kneeled down stuck his tongue inside of her. She jerked with excitement. He allowed her to sit on the edge of the couch and then lock his arms around her thighs so she wouldn't wiggle. This gave her multiple organisms alone. Just when Simone thought that she was incapable of feeling any more pleasure. Steven pushed his manhood inside her. As they moved the rhythm of Mytchel's Carl Thomas CD, Simone felt no guilt. Although, Steven was good at what he did and attempted only to satisfy her, the sex didn't do anything for her. Mytchel still held her heart. When it was over Steven left Simone unsatisfied. Once the charade was over Simone walked Steven to the door and headed straight for the shower. This time the water did nothing for her.

When Two Come Together

Jonathan

"What is with that chic?" Jonathan asked puzzled

"Yea, Meka what is wrong with her?" Mark asked.

"She just broke up with her boyfriend so she a little bit over the edge." Meka explained.

" What did I do?" Jonathan began to look even more confused.

"Probably nothing," Jessica answered. "She'll be okay," She shook her head at the thought of Simone's actions. Mark introduced the girls to Jonathan. The rest of the night was cool. After the club started to die down, they decided to go out for breakfast at IHOP after the club. Jonathan had already made up in his mind that Shanna wasn't a keeper, but she was perfect for one night of pleasure.

Aisha Johnson

When they got back to his apartment, Jonathan advised Shanna to watch her step into the dark apartment. For no reason she giggled. He sat her down on the living room couch and cut the lights on. She was really nervous. " You got any coffee?" She giggled. *Why do they always have to giggle,* Jonathan asked himself.

"Nah, I try to stay away from that stuff." He smiled at her.

"Who is this?" Shanna asked picking up a picture of Tracey.

"That is my ex-girlfriend," he answered, walking into the kitchen.

"Where have I seen her before?" She questioned herself out loud.

"Would you like a soda?" He attempted to change the subject.

"No thanks," she answered. "I know I have seen this girl." She searched her mind harder.

"How could you not know her. She is everywhere these days" Jonathan said in a frustrated tone. Just looking at Shanna he could tell that she would be easy. He walked back over to her pulled the photo out of her hands and placed it back down on the coffee table. He led her back into his bedroom. He cut on a slow cd and turned off the lights. He could tell that Shanna was still nervous so he cut the T.V. on.

"You want to watch Brown Sugar," he asked. She agreed.

When Two Come Together

    They sat on the bed in silence, but only for a short while. Jonathan massaged her thighs every few stokes he moved further up to vagina. Each stoke was constant, until he was massaging it with his fingers. Shanna wanted to be in control and Jonathan was all for that. She pulled out his manhood and began to kiss the tip of it to get him on hard. Then she took off of her panties while instructing him to put on a condom. Although she jumped promptly onto him and rode him like a pro; there was no passion, no zest, and most importantly no love. When it was over Jonathan added her to the list of many who would never receive a phone call.

    As Jonathan sat in his bedroom his mind drifted to the last night that he and Tracey made love. He remembered the intensity. When he made love to women now it was all about him. He could care less about them or there emotions. He decided to call one of the few women in his life that mattered. He looked at his watch and thought now would be a great time to call Australia.

    " Hey this is John," he began.

    "I know who you are, big head." She laughed into the phone. "What's Up?"

    "I am fine and how are you?" Jonathan questioned.

    "I am fine John, however, Tracey is a mess." Tonya explained.

"She will be fine. She didn't take us serious and now she has more time for a career," Jonathan explained to Tonya.

"She took you serious John. She just took her career serious too." Tonya explained.

"I should've been a part of the decision making process" Jonathan continued.

"You're right." Tonya responded. "So, what's going in the N-Y-C? You mean to tell me you don't have a freak over there to keep you warm this late at night?"

"She is already gone home" Jonathan laughed. He talked to Tonya for as long as he could. He loved talking to her. She was the closest female friend he ever had. She was more like his sister than anything else. Tonya, Tony, and Mark had been his friends for as long as he could remember. They grew up in the same neighborhood, went to the same schools and even the same college. Now with different careers they still kept the same friendship. Jonathan decided that it was easier to talk about *her* career and *her* life for the rest of the phone conversation. The truth of the matter was, life without Tracey, was not much to talk about.

When Two Come Together

Simone

Simone use to love New York in the morning. She used to love the crisp air and the busy atmosphere. It always seemed like everyone had somewhere important to go. Today, she hated New York, it seem far too cold and far to busy. As she walked down the busy streets, her mind drifted to Mytchel. God knew she loved that man just as much as she loved New York City. She wondered had there been signs that he was married that she had missed before. She wondered how his wife found out about them? Why hadn't she found out sooner? Simone got to work in no time. She headed to her office to call her grandmother.
    "Hello," Her grandmother answered.

"Hi, Graham," Simone tried to sound happy.

"Hey baby. How are you doing this morning?" She asked Simone.

"I am fine," Simone assured her grandmother. " Did you get that envelope I sent you?" She continued. "I sure did. You know I surely appreciate it," Her grandmother responded.

"How is Mytch?" Graham asked.

"Graham, I don't know. Me and Mytch broke up." Simone began to fight back the tears.

"Well don't worry you are good woman. You are smart and pretty. Whatever you did to him, he will forgive you. Don't worry he will come back." Graham tried to comfort her.

"I don't want him back!" Simone had snapped before she realized it. " I broke up with him " Simone spoke firmly to her grandmother.

"What happened?" Graham sounded surprised.

"Graham, he was married" Simone answered her Grandmother as tears began to wail up in her eyes again.

"How could he have been married?" Her grandmother asked puzzled. For as first time in Simone's life she found her grandmother at a loss of words. "Are you okay?" she finally asked.

"Yea Graham," Simone swallowed hard. "I'm fine." The lie slipped out just as her tears won the battle. Simone was crying again. She knew that breaking off the relationship with Mytch was the best thing to do. She just had no idea how hard it would be.

"Simone, I know that you have Meka and Jessica up there in that city, but you should really think about coming home." Graham always hated the fact that Simone had decided to move up North once she finished college. Although she loved all her grandchildren, Simone was special to her. When Simone's parents died in the car accident, Graham became her mother and father. She always tried to make excuses for Simone to move back to Birmingham.

" Graham, I have to get to work." Simone changed the subject. The two said there goodbyes and Simone checked her morning e-mail. Just as she was about to go down to the vending machine, she was greeted by her boss.

"Hey Mr. G," Simone welcomed him.

"Hi Simone" He smiled back. "Did you look over that software demo cd?" Mr. Grooves asked rubbing his chin.

"Yes I did". Simone answered walking back over to her desk. She sat down and pulled out a folder and handed to him. Here are a few things that I have done with the software. I think we could use this around the office," Simone commented. She could tell by her bosses face that he was extremely pleased. She had forgotten all about the fact that her job was getting new editing software.

Aisha Johnson

"Great," Mr. Groove started to rub his chin again. " I have a meeting with the software designer tomorrow at 12:00. I still haven't decided if this is going to be the software of choice or not. Would you like to join us? We could use a someone as sharp as you are at the meeting on our side."

"Sure" Simone accepted " I'll be there". There had been rumors that Mr. Grooves was looking to promote a photo editor to management. She knew that helping to make decisions like this made increased her chances. *Finally, an excuse to go shopping. 1 Mississippi, 2 Mississippi...*She counted in her head as she watched Mr. Grooves head for the elevator. Within five minutes Simone had packed up her things and fled her office.

Simone walked around Bloomingdales, but she saw nothing that excited her. It was weird She had always went crazy when it came to buying clothes. That was part of the reason why she loved photography so much. She got a chance to create a look. Simone decided to see what Barney's had, but she couldn't find anything there either. Just as she was going to call it a day, she saw a navy blue, Donna Karen power suit in the window of Sax. She ended up buying the shoes, and earrings.

Shopping normally mad her feel better not this time. When she reached her apartment, she rushed to the CD player. She cut on her Jahiem CD and cut on her bath spa. She took a long hot and steamy bath. She lay in the water wishing that

When Two Come Together

Mytch was there to get her out and make love to her. She met Mytchel through her job. Mytchel's company had used Lawson's Marketing and Design to do an international campaign. To celebrate, the company had a big party. *Where was his wife then?* Simone thought to herself. It had never crossed her mind that Mytchel may not have been the one she would spend the rest of her life with. She missed him so much. Yet, there was no way she could forgive him for what he had done.

As she laid in the bathtub her thoughts wondered to the very last time they made love. She remembered him whispering into her ear telling her how much he loved and needed. She remembered the way he moaned with pleasure with each stoke. Simone thoughts were interrupted by the sounds of the telephone.

"Hello", this is Simone," She answered.

"Hi, this is Steven" He sounded nervous.

"Oh," Simone sounded extremely surprised. "Hi" She hadn't remembered giving him her phone number.

"I got your number from the phone book. I hope you don't mind." He began to relax

" Nope, not at all" Simone lied.

" Well, I was wondering if you like to go to lunch or dinner tomorrow?" Steven asked

"I wish I could but I can't," Simone searched her head for the perfect lie. The nerve of him to call. She couldn't believe that he had looked up her number up in the phone book and called.

"Umh- I have a meeting tomorrow and I'm not sure when it will be wrapped up. I also have a lot of work to catch up on." She couldn't come up with a good lie, so she told the truth.

"Okay" He responded. "Well maybe some other time." He managed to say that much.

Simone could tell that his pride was hurt.

"Definitely some other time."

Simone attempted to make him feel better. He was fine and all, but he just wasn't what Simone wanted. First of all, it was way to early for to be thinking about getting involved with anyone. It hadn't even been a full week. Secondly, If she decided to get with someone, they wouldn't have to look her number up in the phone book. The two said their good-byes. Simone enjoyed the rest of her bath.

Later, she laid across her king sized bed thinking of Mytchel. It was only 6:00, and she was all ready for bed. She decided that her self-pity would have to end now. She was no longer going to weep and moan over a married a man. After all, she was a good catch, pretty, smart, employed, no kids, and independent. Simone looked around her bedroom, and it didn't seem as cozy as it once felt. She looked over at her dresser and saw a club flyer on it. Although she was reluctant, she got it and read it. Tonight was open mic night at Nikki's

When Two Come Together

she had never been to one before, she decided to go in and check it out. Simone got dressed, grabbed her journal and left.

    Writing had always been one of Simone's secret passions. She wrote mostly poetry and short stories. Her life was way to busy even think about writing a novel. When she got to Nikki's, it didn't look like the busy club she was use to. There was a real calming vibe. Most of the men and women there wore braids or locs. Each table had burning incense on them. She signed in at the bar like everyone else and sat at a table near the back of the club. She knew that she wouldn't know anyone there. Simone listened to the words of the poet on the stage.

What People Do
You design
Preconceived notions of me
that bring me down
yet somehow
In my sadness
You find your own happiness
You're over critical about my situation
Comments you continuously give
without my invitation
Trying to hurt me
with your intentions dressed up
in deception
as advice

Aisha Johnson
trying to define me
Spreading your false perception
My mind so weak
I am unable to add up my worth
because you're so busy subtracting from me
How will I overcome you
When I don't even know
Who I am
Ashamed of myself
constantly second guessing
myself
Not allowing myself to see past your twisted vision.
Even though I know better
and completely acknowledged your intentions
I gotta to do
better
Once I find me
I should be able to
-Break free

    Simone felt this woman's pain. Each time a new poet came on Simone felt more and more at home. Out nowhere the MC called the next poet.
    "Simone Benson," he looked around in the audience. This was new a poet.
    Simone waited for the girl with same name that she had to walk up to the stage. Silence fell. The MC began to read her address. *Oh my God!* Simone thought to herself. She had signed the

When Two Come Together

sheet to go on to the stage. Already embarrassed Simone grabbed her book and made her way onto the stage. She couldn't believe that she was going to read her words athlete for the first time ever. Butterflies began to form in her stomach as she stared into the crowd of loc's, head wraps, fros and braids that were waiting patiently for her to began. Simone felt the butterflies start to flutter in her stomach. Then a sistah from the audience with an orange afro screamed.

"Take yo- time sistah" As if that statement alone could fix this anxiety.

Then older guy sitting on the other side of the room screamed, "that's right!"

Simone closed her eyes and slung a quick prayer up to the heavens. She swallowed hard and began, to read. She stuttered. " I-I-love" and took and depth breathe and began again

Love

When I was first introduced to you
I was too young to understand
the damage that you could do.
I thought this feeling was so amazing
So easily was I mistaken.
Today you shine bright with good intentions

Aisha Johnson

Tomorrow you rain down with pain.
Now I believe that you are like the snow flakes
that fall
during the winter's storm
unduplicable in design
Yet still the same underline
I don't understand why
each time I came to you
Revealed who I really was to you
allowed you to hear my soul's song
You failed me and left me lonely
though words they often changed
the beats remained the same
No reciprocity ever came
So often I set myself up for love
But love you let me down
With this I became emotionally unstable
Warped myself up in pity
questioned myself
Why should I fall in love again
this proves the old cliché
You don't love nobody anyway
Your ways are so mysterious
so vital to all that is in existence
Without you we are just tingling cymbals
This is in Corinthians
So it's fact not fiction
How does one understand your infinite dimensions
What do we do now
When man takes you for a game

            When Two Come Together
         and uses your name only to gain
         How do we get out of this predicament
         You should be kind, pure, and constant,
                        unconditional
               What is a woman's position
            When she seeks you and doesn't find
                   pretending to be devoted
         but looking at her neighbor with lustful eyes
                 Tell me what should we do
         When all we want is to love and be loved

    Simone closed her eyes and thanked God for the feeling that he left her with. She felt peace of mind. Her soul had been cleansed through the words of poem. She listened for the audience response they all cheered and clapped. Simone made her way back to her seat and listened to more poetry. When it was over, Simone knew that this was where she belonged on Monday nights.

Aisha Johnson

Jonathan

Jonathan hated the subway. He hated to be cluttered under the fat, stinky construction workers. It was even worse when he got stuck sitting next to the little ol' ladies with bad breath who wanted to either tell there life story or hear his. He wanted to buy a car but when the wedding was called off, he had decided that he wouldn't waste his money. It was the 5:30 rush on the subway and there was nowhere for him to sit. His cell phone rang.

"Hello," He answered.

"Hi, Jonathan this is Monica."

"Hi Monica. How can I help you?" The noise from the subway made the cell phone reception horrible, so he just got off.

"Mr. Morris added a noon appointment to your schedule." She explained. "You will be meeting with a Mr. Grooves and Simone Benson. Here are their numbers" Monica gave Jonathan all the information he needed. He walked down to 75th street and decided to go visit his mom. He and his mom were pretty close they normally talked on the phone 3 or 4 times a week. She always made him feel better about the break up. She never liked

Tracey anyway. Besides, he needed his brother to give him a hair cut anyway. Today was one of those days that he would've rather been in bed. At least his mom would be happy to see him. As he made his way down the sidewalk, he stared at all of the kids playing kick ball. They reminded him of the way him and his friends were when they were that age. Why couldn't Tracey be like his mom or most women? Most women wanted a nice house, a nice car and a couple of kids. He could provide that. It didn't matter anyway because Tracey wasn't most women, and she wanted to see the world. The worst part about it all was she wanted someone to trail behind her.

When he reached the gate to the house, he could hear his younger brothers blasting his Cd player louder than his parents would have ever allowed. He walked into the house shocked to find Devin, his younger brother, attempting do his math homework.

"Hey Bro- you must have known I was coming" He slapped his brother on the back of the head. " You can quit pretending to be doing your homework now." He joked.

"What's up Jon man?" His brother spoke back. " I am not pretending," he said getting up to fix himself a cup of kool-aid. "Uncle John said I wouldn't be able to keep cutting hair at the shop if I brought home bad grades, so I got to do, what I got do."

Jonathan was impressed.

"So he finally gave you a chair?"

"Under the condition that my grades are good." Devin replied.

"Congratulations man." Jonathan was extremely proud of his little brother. Devin had been cutting hair since he was 10. Uncle John had forgotten Devin's Christmas present and gave him a pair of clippers one year. Over the last 6 years he had perfected his trade. Sometime between the ages of 13-14 he waited until there Uncle John had gotten sloppy drunk, Devin made him to promise that on his 16th Birthday, he would give him his own chair at the barbershop. Devin was a good barber and Jonathan was a regular customer. So were Mark, Tony and half the neighborhood. The truth was Uncle John needed Devin in that shop although he was ashamed to admit.

"I start Barber College Monday," he said proudly but puzzled at the Math homework in front of him. Jonathan agreed to help his brother with his Math homework in exchange for one last free haircut. He still tipped him $12.00. After the haircut Jonathan decided to walk home he had already endured his share of public transportation for the day. As he walked down the sidewalk, he counted the number of times he saw Tracey face. By the time he crossed the threshold of his apartment, he had decided that it was time to get over Tracey. After all it had been 3 months since

When Two Come Together

they split up. Jonathan walked into his apartment with a frown. He was sick of being lonely. He hated coming home to a dark apartment every night. When he was with Tracey at least she would be there a couple nights a week. The silence and the pain was getting ridiculous. He decided that maybe he needed to see a shrink.

Simone

Simone was excited about her meeting and after the open mic night she felt rejuvenated. She decided to do something different with hair to represent the change that she had decided to make in her life. She called Jessica. " Can you come and put some highlights in my hair?" Simone asked because she knew Jessica wouldn't mind. She had been her and Meka's hair stylist since they were about 10 years old. Jessica could work miracles when came to hair, make-up, and nails. Simone never told Jessica about the open mic night in fact she never told anyone. Simone went to bed early because she wanted to be sure that she was well rested for her meeting tomorrow.

The next morning she was ready to take over the world with her new suit, new hair and new attitude. Simone decided to walk to work she needed to feel the crisp air and see all the busy people walking. Simone arrived at work a little earlier than normal. After sitting down at her desk, she began to check her e-mail. There was one from Mytchel. Simone's instincts told her to delete it but her heart encourage her to read it.

When Two Come Together

Dear Simone,

I want to start off by telling you that every time I told you I loved you it was true.
Every touch and every kiss we shared was real. I know that I lied to you and I know that it was wrong.

She couldn't force herself to continue to read the e-mail so she deleted the email. She had a business meeting in a few hours and didn't need the thought of a cheater lingering on her mind. Simone felt herself about to have a break down. The phone rang.
"Simone Benson," she tried to sound as professional as possible.
"Hello, this is Jonathan Williams from EditCorp. I was calling to see if you needed to see a presentation before we went out for our lunch meeting? Jonathan questioned. *"Was that the voice of a sistah?"* Jonathan asked himself.
"If you have time, I would really appreciate it." Simone answered. I have done a few things with the software but I still have a lot of questions that you may be able to iron out for me." Simone began to smile.
"What time is good for you? " Jonathan asked.

"Anytime. " Simone answered. " I am here now," She flirted.

"I can be there in to 10 minutes." He flirted back.

Editcorp, as a whole, shocked Simone. First, they had a great product. Secondly, they had excellent customer service. Most software companies send you the product and you either like it or you don't. Simone went back into her folder and reviewed the work that she had done. She also took another look at the trial disk to see if she had any technical questions. She wanted to be well prepared for the meeting so she facilities to get a conference room. Then she sent her intern to grab fresh doughnuts from across the street and on a fresh pot of coffee. She also called Mr. Grooves to see if he would be attending the meeting and learned that had taken the morning off and would not be in until later that afternoon.

Jonathan

Jonathan made his way to his appointment. He normally liked to show up early but right on time would have to do. Simone Benson it sounded like a black name, but her voice threw him off. He hardly ever met women photo editors.
Black or white, she sure sounded sexy.
When he got to her office she had stepped out but her intern seated him in her office. Looking around her office he could tell she was black. She had pictures of her along with the hottest clothing designers and models in the fashion industry.

"Hello, Mr. Williams. I am sorry I kept you waiting," she extended her hand for a proper handshake.

"It was no problem at all." He shook her hand.

"I have a conference room all set up. If you'll follow me." Simone led Jonathan into the conference room. Although, there were only two people in the conference room, they maintained the presentation at a professional level. Jonathan was really nervous. Then it hit him, he knew her from somewhere. He searched his mind over a thousands times, but just couldn't remember where he knew her from. After the power point presentation was complete, Jonathan opened the floor for questions.

"Mr. Williams, I will be honest with you. I love your software. However, I do have a few concerns. In our line of work we can't afford to be down for too long. How long is it going to take to get the software up and get out to the staff fully operational." Simone questioned.

"It won't take us any longer that 48 hours. We also do upgrades and up-training at reduced costs." Jonathan assured Simone.

He could tell by her facial expression that the software had her approval. Just as they were closing the meeting Mr. Grooves walked into the conference room. Simone promised to deliver him a typed report before lunch.

When Two Come Together

Jonathan caught Simone walking back to her office.

"Excuse me," he rushed over to her. " This might sound crazy, but I am sure that we have met before."

"How sure are you?" Simone asked. Jonathan could tell by the look in her eyes that she knew exactly where they had met. Jonathan was speechless, so he decided to just smile. When they reached her office Simone invited him in and closed the door.

"Real sure," he flirted back.

"What does it matter?" Simone questioned, as she sat down at her desk.

"It doesn't. I really just want to get to know you better" Jonathan grinned.

"When I tell you when and where we met, how do you know that you will still want to get to know me better?" Simone smiled as she logged into her work computer.

"Unless we are related, I am sure" Jonathan answered.

"I am embarrassed to say." Simone looked at Jonathan.

"Why?" Jonathan asked puzzled.

"A couple days ago, at Nikki's, I went off on you for making me spill my Margarita. I am sorry" Simone sounded genuinely sorry.

"Oh that's right. I remember now. Yea your hair is different." Jonathan recalled. He pulled out his business card and wrote his mobile number and home number on the back. "I'll let you make that up to me." He handed her the card with a devilish look on his face.

"Really, when?" Simone asked, while looking down at the card.

" Tonight over dinner at LaShunda's," He answered.

Simone agreed. The lunch meeting went great and for the first time since Jonathan's break-up with Tracey, he decided to get to know someone. He couldn't put his finger on it, but he was feeling Simone. After dinner, they went back up to her place. The night ended with a simple good bye. As Jonathan walked home, he reflected over the fun he had with Simone. It had been a long time since he so much fun. For the first time in a long time, Jonathan went to sleep with a woman other than Tracey on his mind. The next morning Jonathan decided he would catch a cab. It looked like it could rain any second.

"What are you doing here?" Simone leaned on the frame of the door. Sipping a up of hot tea.

"Just loading some software. I will be here for the next 3 or 4 days. I am going to be teaching a few training classes on the software as well." He could tell by Simone's facial expression that she was glad that he would be around. He wanted to ask her out to lunch, but didn't want to crowded her space. Just as he finished loading the new

When Two Come Together

software on her computer, Simone invited him over to her apartment for dinner. Jonathan agreed. It was weird how that one dinner led to another. Before he knew it, 2 months had one by since they had started dating. They went to the movies, the park, a few plays, concerts, shopping, basketball games, and dancing. Things were looking up. Jonathan rarely ever thought about Tracey any more.

Simone

Simone stood in the mirror putting the finishing touches on her make-up. She couldn't believe that her and Jonathan had been dating now for 2 months. It had been great. Tonight, for the first time, she was going to let him go to Nikki's Open Mic night with her. She had been going now since before they met. She was sure to never miss a meeting. Getting up on stage reading her poetry did wonders for her soul.
There was knock at the door she assumed it was Jonathan.
She walked towards the door, but it was unlocked and Mytchel just walked right in.
 " Hey, you miss me?" He managed to say. Simone could smell the beer on him from across the room.
 " Mytchel, what's wrong?" She asked puzzled but concerned
 " She finally left me." He flopped down on Simone's couch.
 "After all these years, she finally let me go. She took my baby too." Simone watched his eyes tear up. "When you and I were dating, I begged her to leave me. She said that I was just amusing myself with you since, I had been with her for so

When Two Come Together

many years. She said it was natural for a man to cheat."

A silence fell over the room and the emotions got thick. Tears were streaming down his face. Simone had never seen Mytchel cry or get drunk. Mytchel broke the silence. "She hooked up with some doctor at the hospital she worked with." Although, Simone understood Lisa and believed that she should have let him a long time ago. She felt sorry Mytchel. " Simone, you know I loved you. I still love you." Simone felt like she had to hold him and be there for him in his time of need. She pulled him close and began to comfort him in his ear. She told him that everything was going to be okay.

He wrapped his arms around her and kissed her on her neck. He moved down to her chest. Never missing a beat with the intent to please. A part of Simone wanted to stop him but she couldn't. This was Mytchel, the person who knew her body like no one else did. Within seconds he had undone her robe and laid her out on the bare carpet. He undressed himself quickly. Simone stared at his perfect body. He allowed his hands to feel her wetness. He blew on her womanhood, causing her to shiver. He kissed what he felt would always belong to him. Simone anticipation grew. Just as he was about go inside her the phone rung.

"Wait!" Simone jumped up and headed to pick the phone up. She finally realized what she was about to do. "Hello," she answered.

"Hey baby, I'll be there in a second. I am sorry that we are running late. If you are dressed and ready to go, then we can just take this cab on over" Jonathan sounded excited.

"That way we won't be late"

"I am ready."

Simone lied as she stared down on her naked body.

"I'll be downstairs waiting."
Simone made her way back to the living room.

"Mytch, you know I can't do this." Simone said softly while tears began to fill her eyes.

"Simone, you're going to send me away just like that?" Mytchel asked, baffled

"You made me the other woman. I thought we had a future together and your sorry ass was already married. Anyway, more importantly, I have a man now." Simone explained proudly as Jonathan came to her mind.

"He ain't got shit on me!" Mytchel yelled and moved in closer. " He will never have shit on me!" He reached for Simone. She jerked back.

"No Mytchel, leave. She walked to the door and motion for him to get out. As she got dressed, she thought about what Mytchel had said. The truth was, Simone didn't know what it felt like to be with Jonathan. She could only imagine when and

When Two Come Together

what it was going to be like. Of course they had came really close a more than one occasion, but something had always interrupted. In all honesty, Simone was getting frustrated. There was a plus side to all of it, though. With Jonathan, there was a mental connection. This connection was something she had never experienced before, and it felt good.

Aisha Johnson

Jonathan

Simone didn't look like the poetic type. She had never let him hear or read any of her poetry before, but he was still very excited. He would have never even known that she wrote if that weird looking lady with orange hair hadn't came over to the table during dinner, the other night and talk to her about her poetry. Although, her hated to admit it, he did not like the fact that, he had to practically invite himself. Simone didn't normally hold things in or back so why was this any different. When he pulled up to the apartments, she was waiting, but could tell something was bothering her. Jonathan figured she was probably just nervous.

"You look beautiful." He whispered in Simone's ear, as kissed her cheek. It was when she looked like this that he wanted to take her back to his place and put it on her. He was just unsure how

When Two Come Together

to approach the situation. When they first started dating, she had told him how she had just got of a long-term relationship. He wasn't really sure where they stood. She had initially told him that she needed some time. Of course the fact that they had been dating almost 3 months and had not had sex bothered him. He had just decided that he would let her make the first move. Simone was special to him and he wasn't going to ruin it.

When they walked in the door a lot of people smiled and spoke to Simone. Some hugged her, while others nodded their head up to acknowledge her. The vibe in the room was so different that Jonathan forgot that they were at Nikki's. It even looked different. He sat down next to Simone. The first poet to get up was the lady with the orange hair.

Our Journey

I remember when we first met
It was a Saturday.
How could I forget
No wait, my bad.
A Sunday morning
You were sitting directly
in front of me.
On the bus. (Do you remember?)
I kept my crush.
on you secret

Aisha Johnson
but you knew
didn't you?
That I had feelings bottled up inside
I couldn't hide
Even when I was dating that other guy
You've got to admit
I tried.
Remember those mornings before school
when we would talk on the phone.
Or the late night conversations
after the three-way conversations with him
it was on
But we were only kids then
look how many years ago that's been
We are grown now
and we can do
whatever it is we want to
we are only miles apart
So there no excuse
this can go as far as we choose
What's funny is even then I knew you were the truth
I could tell by the way you made me feel
I pleaded myself to be happy with the one
I was with
But you were always in the background
My bonus, my free gift. (are you smiling?)
intelligent, sexy, strong and I even loved your cologne.

When Two Come Together

I saved myself in hopes that you would be the one
who made me moan.
Well like I said
that was then
and this is now
or forever
whatever
we choose.

Jonathan could tell that the poem was about the man that was sitting at the next table. After every couple of lines he would say something to confirm it. The next poet got up and said that her poem was dedicated to all the men who she had turned down over the last couple of years.

Superstar

When those young girls
look at you
they see all the things
they want in a man
you got rims
and those new Timberlands
When they see the way your

Aisha Johnson
jewelry blings
Those girls fall down at your knees
So you're a superstar
it seems
You got braids
and those shades
with smooth chocolate skin
that's why they give in
The way you cruise around town
shows you enjoy your status as a star
And who can blame you
for that
but please keep your game back
Because being a superstar
just isn't enough for me
I know you got money
But I need more
A sun
or a king
Your style is digital
but your spirit ain't free
I need someone who can really make me happy

    Jonathan was shocked that he wasn't bored out of his mind. The MC called Simone. She kissed him on his cheek and made her way on stage. *God she is beautiful.* Jonathan thought to himself as we watched her.

When Two Come Together

"This poem is dedicated to the guy in the back." As the words rolled off of her tongue Jonathan heart started to beat extremely fast.

What is This?

Last night,
For the very first time,
I looked into your eyes,
What is this????
I asked myself as chills began to roll down my spine.
I am having thoughts of making you mine.
But I don't know if that is wise
I just keep thinking you could be God's beautiful surprise,
'Cause what else could this be?
Could you be the one
He made especially for me?
I guess only time will allow us to see.
For some reason
I feel compelled to share with you,
All my dreams and bare my soul to you.
I feel that you are the truth.

Aisha Johnson

And so I am trusting you without any proof.
It all just happened so fast,
I'm wondering if this will last.
Let's put away each other's past,
And work on a future
Could it be lust?
I think not,
even though you went directly to my spot
and had me all hot.
Your conversation elevated me
Your words spoke pleasure to me
So what could this be???????
I could be the one for you
or Could it be I am just one of the chosen few
You choose to improve
before you leave this earth
If that is so I wait patiently
for the lesson I am about receive
I looked in your eyes
right after the first kiss
and I caught a glimpse of happiness
So what is this???????

Simone was a great poet. Her words had grabbed Jonathan and taken him on an emotional roller coaster. When she was done, people stood up and began to clap. Jonathan saw a special peace cover her face when she sat back down at the table. He smiled to himself, because he knew exactly what "this" was. It couldn't be anything

When Two Come Together

other than love. Instead of going back to his place as planned, the lady with orange hair, Deborah, and her husband, Earl, invited them over to their table. Before they realized it the night had slipped away. With work tomorrow, Simone went her way and Jonathan went his. The rest of the week was pretty hectic Jonathan had won 3 new clients, and Simone was working on an ad for a large retail store. They next date wasn't set until Friday night. The night of Tonya's sister party.

Aisha Johnson
Simone

The week went by pretty quickly. Simone had some last minute shopping to do for the party. As, she and Meka walked around the Victoria Secrecy's, looking for the perfect set to go up under her new dress for the party she and Jonathan were going to. Simone was exited about meeting all of his friends.

"Ok Meka, I'm fed up" Simone told her cousin in a frustrated voice. "It will be three months on Wednesday, and we still haven't done it."

"Why don't you make the first move?" Meka suggested.

"I can't make the first move on the first time," Simone argued. " I'd look desperate."

"You are desperate," Meka laughed.

"Whatever!" Simone tried to laugh it off knowing it was the truth. Tonight was the night that she was hell bent on getting some.

"You better act fast for one of those models at that party act sooner, " Ta Meka warned holding up and lace pink set. Simone nodded in disapproval.

"You know what?" She paused. "You are right." Simone shuffled through her purse to find her cell phone. She dialed Jonathan's number.

"Hey Baby," he answered.

When Two Come Together

"Hey John," Simone smiled at her cousin. "I was just thinking that since I am going to have to share you with all your friends tonight would it be possible for you to get dressed at my apartment tonight?"

"Sure." Jonathan answered without even pondering the question. "I'll be there around six, is that okay?"

"Yea sure," Simone agreed looking at her watch. The two said there good-byes and Simone looked back up at her cousin Ta Meka.

"Damn Simone, I said make the first move. Don't beg for the shit." Ta Meka laughed and walked away.

"Fuck you," Simone laughed. She bought five new bra sets. She figured that she should be prepared for a weekend of good fun. The time passed slowly. Simone decided to pull out her poetry journal to work on some new stuff for open mic night. Then, at exactly 6:00, Jonathan knocked on the door. A nervousness fell over Simone.

"Hey," Simone smiled once she finally opened the door with only her robe on.

Aisha Johnson

Jonathan

When Jonathan arrived at Simone's apartment he could tell she was nervous but he also knew that the time was right. *Finally* He thought to himself. He looked Simone over with lustful eyes, she was beautiful. He had been waiting on this moment so long that he didn't know where to start.

"Let me show you where to put your bags." Simone led him into her bedroom. Jonathan dropped his bags at the foot of the bed. He hung his tux up on her door.

"Would you like some tea?" Simone asked nervously.

"No thanks," Jonathan began to get a little nervous too.

"Well, can I get you anything?" Simone asked as she walked backwards toward the door.

"Umh," Jonathan swallowed hard. "Yea, you," he smiled. He walked over to Simone and grabbed her by her hips and pulled her close to him. Simone could feel his hard on. She closed her eyes and bit her lip as Jonathan moved from her neck to her

When Two Come Together

breast with his tongue. Within seconds the nervousness left the room. Simone and Jonathan were filled with passion. They both had been waiting for what seemed like eternity for this moment.

    Jonathan removed Simone's robe and laid her on her bed. Her heart was beating so fast, so loud, Jonathan allowed it to guide their rhythm. He slid his finger inside of her. She jerked and let out a premature moan. She was wet, warm, and ready. He licked every inch of her body. Kissing her in places that no other man had ever thought needed attention. Simone was no novice. She eased her hand down to penis and kissed and massaged it. She used her hands and lips and sucked it in such a way Jonathan had to battle with his organism. A few seconds slow and then a few seconds fast. This was pleasure. He rubbed his manhood up and down the split of her vagina, this caused the jewel between her legs to throb with anticipation. Simone couldn't take it for long, at a heighten moment, she nudged her left hip and he was inside of her. They moved hard and fast with no condom. They couldn't stop. He was far too firm and she was far too wet. He looked in Simone's face, the need for control filled her eyes. He gave way to the demands of her eyes. Suddenly, Simone was on top. He was holding her by her firm hard breast. She was riding him like a pro. Then from nowhere Jonathan pushed Simone up and flipped her over. He mounted her. Then by using her shoulders, to thrust himself in side her, he took control. As he spanked her, she moaned, because this was good lovin. When he was about to release his love juices, he wanted to look in her eyes so he laid her on her back.

He wanted to look in her eyes during the last few minutes of his pleasure. The first stroke was what did it for Simone this wasn't an ordinary release for her. The ball of stress that was relived flowed smoothly like a Tennessee River. Jonathan could feel this and it weakened him. The second stroke was all it took his love juices were spilled. They both lay tired, hot, and sweaty. When it was over, Jonathan just laid inside of her. He could was still feeling her throbbing. It was if there bodies were in deep conversation. Simone broke the silence.

"Jonathan can you spend the night?" Simone asked.

"Yea baby" Jonathan answered as he stroked Simone's hair. Maybe now was a good time to tell her how he felt. "Baby come on, lets get up I don't want to be late." Maybe not

Simone got up and took a shower first. As they scrambled around her apartment to get dressed they laughed and talked about their day. Once they were booth completely ready to go Jonathan grabbed Simone by the arm and walked

When Two Come Together

her back into the bedroom. They walked out on the balcony. "Simone Benson I love you" the words seem to roll of his tongue so easily. Jonathan felt great. There once was a time in his life when thought he wouldn't be able to feel that way.

"I love you too" Simone kissed her man under the moonlight.

The cab ride was pretty short. He watched Simone stare out into the window and wondered what she was thinking. Jonathan was surprised at Simone's level of the game. She had let go of the shy role early and had proved to be a treat in bed. He had couldn't wait to show off to his boys. He knew once they met her that they would understand why he his he was over Tracey. When they entered the party Jonathan's friends hurried over.

Simone

When they walked into the ballroom Simone was in awe of how beautiful the room was. When they walked into the room it seemed like Jonathan was the guest of honor. Simone watched as Jonathan interacted with his friends.

"What's up" a guy asked as he shook Jonathan's hand. "You must be Simone." he smiled.

"Yea." Simone had eased back into her shy mode and forced out a smile.

"This is Mark and his wife Shannice." Jonathan introduced them, greeting Shannice with a kiss on the cheek.

"Yea, you work with my cousin Ta Meka, Ta Meka McDaniels," Simone recalled.

"That is me," Mark put on his boyish grin.

"Hey guys." Another guy walked over to them.

"What's up Tony?" Jonathan asked.

"Nothing much," Jonathan answered.

"Simone, this is Tony" He introduced them.

Simone could tell that Tony was checking her out.

"Hi." She decided not to look at him.

"It is really nice to meet you," Tony said looking up from her butt, as he secretly gave Jonathan the seal of approval.

When Two Come Together

"Excuse me, can I get a little attention?" The woman had walked into the middle of the circle. Simone had seen pictures of Tonya before, but they really didn't her any justice she was a beautiful woman. Everyone hugged her and kissed her.

"You must be Simone?" She smiled. Simone nodded shyly.

"It is so nice to finally meet you. For a minute, we thought Jonathan had made you up."

Everyone in the group laughed. They huddled for a few seconds and then kind of scattered on there own way.

"You didn't tell me that Tony and Tonya were twins." Simone interrupted Jonathan's thoughts.

"I think sometimes I forget" Jonathan said in his defense to Simone. He pulled her out onto the dance floor. As they danced, Simone's mind drifted back to the love making that had taken place. She wondered was his stamina the result of the three months of celibacy, or was he always delivering like that. She closed her eyes as her mind wondered back to how he had pleased her with his tongue. As the music continued Jonathan held Simone closer and tighter. She felt safe, secure and loved in his arms. When the song went off they made there way to an empty table. As soon as they got seated and comfortable, Tony walked over to the table.

"Do you mind if I steal him for second?" He asked

"Nah, I think I'm gonna go to freshen up anyway" Simone answered getting up from the table. She walked through the crowed party with confidence, even though the room was filled with some of the most beautiful women in the world. Simone felt beautiful and strong.

When Two Come Together
Jonathan

When Simone left the table they both watch fad into the crowed. "So what do you think?" Jonathan waited on his friend's approval.

"She is a dime, but Tracey is here," Tony warned his friend.

"Damn," Jonathan got a frustrated look on his face.

" I just thought I would give you the heads up" Tony smiled and walked away.

Jonathan went back to his table. Tonight was definitely not the night for her to pop in the picture. She was supposed to be France. He never would've thought that she would be here. *What did it matter?* He tried to convinced himself. He was here with Simone the woman of his dreams. He had originally said no drinking tonight, but he had to get something in his system now. He grabbed a glass of Champaign form one the waiters walking by. All he could think was *damn, damn, damn.*

"Hey handsome," a voice called out from behind him. He knew that voice from anywhere.

"Hello Tracey," he responded without turning around.

"Can I sit down?" She walked over to a chair at the table.

"Please don't," he said with no emotions at all.

" I have been gone for 5 months. Can I at least get a hug?"

"NO," Jonathan stood up to walk away. Tracey grabbed him by the arm." I know that you are here with some little hussy" She smiled. " I am not trying to ruin that."

Jonathan took a deep breath. "Then what do you want?" He asked frustrated.

"I just want to talk" She let his arm go. " I missed you. Aren't you going to even ask how I am doing? Didn't you even miss me?"

"Nope! Who gives a damn weather or not I missed you. I know I don't care whether or not you missed me." Jonathan answered. "If either of us gave a damn, we would be celebrating a wedding or baby right now."

"It's not to late" Tracey tried to reassure him. When she saw Simone walking back over to them. Tracey moved in kissed him. She pushed her cold tongue down his throat. He jumped back but it was to late Simone had already seen it.

When Two Come Together

Simone

As Simone walked back over to the table, she could see the two of them talking. She couldn't make out what she was saying. She didn't recognize her as Jonathan ex-girlfriend the super model. Then it happened, the kiss.

"Jonathan!" Simone managed to squeeze out. Simone grabbed her purse and coat and headed for the door. There was no way she was going to forget her purse this time. She could hear Jonathan in the background calling her name. She didn't want to look at him. All she could think about was the how things went down with Mytchel. Simone couldn't take another

"I did it for the kid's story." Her head was spinning. She was on the verge of a break down. She couldn't believe that this was happening to her all over a again. She hailed a cab and went straight back to her apartment. She couldn't look at the City of New York right now, it seem to be the city of betrayal. Just as she was walking up the steps, she felt her phone vibrate. There were 5 new messages. She figured that they were all from Jonathan. When she got to the door, there was a note from Ta Meka. It said that there grandmother had been rushed to Brook Green Medical Center. Simone did everything she could to hold things together. She called Meka, and both her and Jessica came up to her apartment.

"What is wrong with Graham?" Simone asked with tears streaming down her face.

"She had a stroke." Jessica answered.

Simone couldn't hold it together anymore. Her biggest fear was losing her grandmother. TaMeka and Jessica's eyes were blood shot red from all the crying they had done. They watched as Simone, who was often the strongest link, broke. She lay in the floor of her apartment in a $200.00 dress. She was broken hearted and afraid. She prayed to God for strength and courage to pull things back together.

When Two Come Together

Simone got up from the floor and used the same scissors she had used to cut off the tags off the dress, to cut the dress down the center. As she changed into her jeans she told TaMeka to book them on the next available flight. She ordered Jessica to call the airport in Birmingham and reserved them a car to drive. Simone fixed some hot tea and began to pack her clothes. The phone kept ringing. Frustrated, Simone unplugged it. Ta Meka informed that they were scheduled to leave in 2 hours. Once they finished packing they headed straight to the airport.

The cab ride was silent. Once they reached the airport, Simone went into a little shop and bought tons of magazines, and snacks for her cousins. She wanted to keep them as quiet as possible. She didn't want them to ask her about the party. She wasn't ready to talk about it just yet. She wasn't sure what had happen. Who was the lady kissing Jonathan. She wanted to talk to Jonathan first. She just couldn't talk to him tonight. She had to focuses on her grandmother. As the women waited on their plane, Jessica decided to try to make small talk to lighten the mood.

"Aren't you going to tell us about your night." She questioned, Simone.

"How could you be thinking about that at a time like this" Simone snapped.

Aisha Johnson

"Simone, the doctor said that Graham is going to pull through" Meka assured her cousin. Simone reached in her bag and pulled out one of her favorite CD's and headsets. She placed them over her ears and closed her eyes. She wanted to cry, but she couldn't. Simone was all cried out, so let the music take her away. When they boarded the plan, she handed out magazines, snacks, and gum to Jessica and Simone. She pulled out her journal and began to write. Writing couldn't ease the pain of her broken heart, it only allowed her to explore deeper into her emotions. Simone couldn't sleep. She just let the plane take her way. Once they finally reached Alabama Simone started to feel a little better. They picked up their rental car and headed to their grandmothers house. As they rode through Smith End Estates, memories of Simone's childhood fill her head. She smiled as she realized she missed the innocence of Birmingham.

When Two Come Together

Jonathan

"Damn Tracey," Jonathan yelled in anger. He jerked back. It was too late Simone had already seen it and was on her way out the door. He tried to follow her, but she hailed a cab. Jonathan went back into the party to say goodbyes and to get his things. He tried Simone on her cell phone a few times, but she didn't answer. She wouldn't answer her home phone either, so he went by her apartment. There was no one there. He went downstairs to Ta Meka's apartment and got no answer. He couldn't remember which apartment belonged to Jessica so he knocked on all three doors on that end of the hall. A teenager pointed him into the right direction. No one was there either. He wasn't up for another cab ride so he walked back to his apartment.

Aisha Johnson

How could he have hurt Simone? He loved her. How could he have let her slip through his fingers so easily? He stood at his door and frowned at the thought of entering his apartment alone. He pulled out a beer from his refrigerator and turned on his CD player. He sat on his couch in the dark. Hoping that the darkness would hide his tears. Simone could have easily been the one. His phone rang. He didn't even bother to answer it. He knew that it wasn't Simone. He just listened to answering machine.

"This is Tonya. I know you are there, pick up the phone." Jonathan didn't budge.

"I know what Tracey did, Jonathan. In her defense, she loves you." Tonya reasoned with the answering machine. "You guys belong together." Jonathan held his middle finger up at the answering machine. " Simone is a nice and pretty girl." Tonya continued. "But face it, she's not Tracey." Tonya finally stop talking and Jonathan got up to unplug the answering machine in the dark. There was knock at the door.

"Jonathan" Tracey called out to him." I know you are in there." He could hear the frustration in her voice.

He walked over to the door and cracked it. " If you know me so well, why don't you know that I don't want to be bothered with your ass," he said firmly.

When Two Come Together

"Jonathan, let me in," she said frustrated. She pushed passed the door and flicked on the lights.

"First of all, don't make this my fault." She said putting her over night bag down and walking over to his refrigerator.

"What do you mean don't make this your fault?" Jonathan looked confused. He wanted to hit her. *Why did she bring clothes?*

"Who told you to show up at my best friends welcome home party with a tramp?" Tracey yelled.

"Tracey you know you are a real piece of work. Why did you bring an overnight bag? You thought you could come over here and I would just fuck your brains out. Then next week it would be all about your career. I-" Jonathan snapped. Before he could get out another word. Tracey threw her hand up and interrupted.

"Hold up. It's okay for you to put time and effort in your career, but I can't put it into mine? Jonathan, I never made you chose between me and *your* career. It's not fair for you to want me to choose," Tracey rebutted.

"Whatever! I wanted you to be my wife. I wanted you to be beside me for the rest of my life. You wanted to be in front of a camera. Those two things just don't mix. Here I am finally starting over. I finally met someone who I think I could be with, and you fuck that up." Jonathan yelled

"Please! That girl ain't got shit on me John and you know it." Tracey boasted.

"You are stupid, you know that? You want me to fuck you?" He shouted angrily.

Tracey looked him in eyes and answered as if they weren't in the middle of an argument. "That's what I am here for" She said innocently. "I need you to make love to me." She walked over to him and rubbed his chest he jerked back.

Jonathan's anger took over him. His heart was hurting so bad it hard to breathe. He led Tracey back into his bedroom. He knew that having sex with her would not do nothing for the pain he felt. He just hoped that it would take his mind off Simone long enough to breathe. Just as she about to get undressed, he stopped her. He turned her around and grabbed a condom out of his nightstand drawer. He bent her over in the doggy position. He used his hand slide her thong over to one side. He forced his penis inside her no four play. She wasn't ready, but he didn't care. He fucked her dry. He pushed himself in out hard and fast as if it were a race. As she moaned with pleasure, She started to get wet and excited. He frowned with disgust. She wasn't the same woman he had once loved. He could tell that she had been with other men because the fit was no longer perfect. She had become one of those women he would add to the list of never getting a call back. She wanted to

When Two Come Together

turn around and look at him. He refused. When it was over tried to kiss him. He refused.

"Tracey you don't get it do you. I just fucked you. I didn't make love to you. We are not the same two people we use to be. Get out of my apartment."

"So it's like that John?" Tracey tried to control her tears, as she scrambled to get her things. Jonathan didn't even look at her. When she walked towards the door, she waited on him to try to stop her.

"You got what you came here for, you have been fucked. Now go back to France." He pushed her out of the door and slammed it behind her.

Aisha Johnson
Simone

When they reached her grandmother's house, Simone located the key to the house key on her key ring. She rubbed it, remembering when she tried to give it back before she left for New York, her grandmother had said that no matter what this house would always be her home.

Simone headed straight for her old room. Everything was just the way she left. When she wasn't there her grandmother would just close the door. As she flopped down on her old bed, she finally understood what her grandmother meant. This was home. Ta Meka and Jessica took their showers, while Simone began to clean. She washed the dishes, swept and mopped the floor. She made up her Grandmother's bed. Then she pulled out the old, big, blue, bible that her Grandmother used to always read to her to comfort her in her time of need back in the day. Whether it would be a bad dream, broken toys, grades, boys her grandmother taught her to seek comfort in Gods word.

Finally, all three of the ladies had showered and were ready to go. They headed to the hospital. Simone hated hospitals. She couldn't help it. This was the same hospital that her parents were rushed to the night that they died. She couldn't believe that she was there again. Fear began to

When Two Come Together

take over her body. Jessica had called in advance to get all the information on her grandmother, so it was just a matter of finding room 247. On their way to their grandmother's room they ran into Jessica's mother. She hugged her daughter and nieces. "If I would've known that a stroke would have brought you girls back to Alabama, I would have had one a long time ago." She joked. She looked at Simone's face and saw her pain.

"Simone, don't worry. Gina Mae is fine." She tried to comfort her niece. Simone walked on into the hospital room, while Jessica and Meka talked to Jean. The room was so cold and dark, the way she felt about New York when she fled the party. Without saying a word she opened all the blinds in the room.

"Simone," her grandmother managed to mumble. The sunlight made the room look and feel so much better.

"Yes Ma'am" Simone smiled at her grandmother.

"Do you need an extra blanket?" Simone said searching through the closets of the hospital room.

"No," her grandmother attempted to speak again. Simone opened up her bag and pulled out the big blue bible. Then she slid her shoes off and climbed in the bed next to her grandmother. She prayed before she opened it. Once she opened her eyes, she began to read to her grandmother.

Within the next 20 minutes her grandmother was sound asleep.

When her cousins came in the room they decided no to disturb their grandmother. Simone had a few words with the doctor and they all head back to her Grandmother's house.

Now that Simone knew that everything was alright with her grandmother, she wanted to call Jonathan but she didn't know what to say. She decided that she needed to clear her head. So she did what she always did when her mind got cluttered, she ran. As Simone ran around her old neighborhood she thought about New York. The cold weather, the high cost of living, and the low down, dirty men. Then she began to think of Alabama. Alabama had the best weather, and it was dirt cheap to live in Hover Field, which was one of the best neighborhoods in town.

The men here were still low down but she had to admit the good out weighed the bad. That's when Simone decided that she was moving back to Alabama. She didn't want to say anything right away. She wanted to be sure that she wasn't acting out anger or fear. She headed home and took a shower. She was going to call Jonathan but she couldn't. Simone was ready to talk to him. In all honesty, she didn't know what to say to him. What kind of questions would she ask him? What was there to talk about? The only thing Simone was

When Two Come Together

sure about was the pain. She decided that instead of calling Jonathan, she needed to go to sleep.

Aisha Johnson

Jonathan

It had been week and a half, and he couldn't get in touch with Simone. He went to her job, her apartment, and even open mic night. I seemed as though she had vanished. He missed her so much. He didn't want to eat or sleep. After leaving her apartment for the fifth time, he decided to stop by his parent's house.

"Hello" Jonathan his mother opened the door. And led him into the kitchen where she was cooking spaghetti.

"Hey Ma," he spoke and kissed her on the cheek." Where is pop?"

"He's down stairs watching the news."

"Oh, So how is everything going?" His mother questioned.

"I am fine, but what is wrong with you son?" She wiped her hands on a towel and sat down at the table next him.

"Nothing Ma," He lied.

"You are my child. I had you. I was in labor with you for 21 hours. I see the trouble in your eyes, so what is bothering you?" His mother confronted him.

"Tracey is back in town, and Simone saw Tracey kiss me at Tonya's party. Now she won't

When Two Come Together

answer any of my calls. I can't get in touch with her or anything. I've been to her job, her apartment, and this little open mic night she goes to. It's like she just vanished or something. Ma, I love her." Jonathan let the words spill like a can beans.

"Son, I tried to tell you back when you first started dating that girl that she was no good for you," his mother got angry.

"I know Ma, and I should have listened" He agreed

"So what are you going to do?" His mother asked " Simone seems like a nice girl. She really cares about you. I can see it in her eyes." His mother continued. His mom had only seen Simone a couple of times. He had taken Simone to the Church picnic one weekend when they had first started dating. She had also stopped by the barber shop with him one day while his parents were up there. His family liked Simone a lot she even let Devon arch her eyebrows.

"That is just it," Jonathan said frustrated. "There isn't much I can do. I can't find her. I've been to her job, her apartment, and her friends apartment I can't find her" He and his mother talked a little while longer and Jonathan caught the subway home. He was lonely and today he wouldn't have mind a little old lady with bad breath that wanted to hear his story. Instead, he got stuck between two fat construction workers.

When he reached his apartment building, he saw Tracey on the steps.

"Why are you here?" Jonathan asked her with no emotion.

" I am here to apologize" She answered. He could tell that she had been crying.

"Come on up" he led Tracey up to his apartment and offered her a soda.

"John when I took that job, I knew you were mad at me. I knew that I had hurt you. I didn't know that you were fed up with me. I didn't know that I couldn't make you happy anymore." Tracey confessed.

"How could you have thought that I would just take that?" He looked puzzled.

" You told me the first time I went out of town on a shoot if the love is real. It will be here when I got back. I believed that and every photo shoot I went on I remembered that." She wiped her tears. " This time when I came back, I expected the love to be here waiting on me. I knew that what we shared was real." She explained to him.

Jonathan looked at Tracey and he understood her pain. "Tracey, I am in love with Simone." He saw his words cut through Tracey's heart like a knife. He hated that things had turned out this way for them. He felt bad about the fact that he had disrespected her body. How he had mishandled her. He never thought in million years that the love

When Two Come Together

they once shared would have came to this. They talked a little while longer about what happened, and why. When she left, he felt like he was finally truly over her.

Aisha Johnson
Simone

The two weeks flew, by and Graham was home safe and sound. People crowded the house all day and evening visiting either Graham and the girls. Simone missed Jonathan so much that she finally called and checked her messages. A few people from the Open Mic night had called to see why Simone was out. As much as Simone hated to admit it; it was time to head back to New York. So a couple of days later, her and cousins headed back. She had decided she would at least wait until December to even consider moving back. She wanted to give her grandmother some time to heal. The flight back to New York was nothing like the flight to Alabama. The girls laughed and talked. Simone finally told her cousins what happen between her and Jonathan.

"Simone, why didn't you ask what the hell was going on" Jessica asked. "You are one of the strongest women I know but when it comes to men you have a way of backing down, why?"

"It didn't matter what was going on. All I needed to know, I saw with my own two eyes" Simone defended her actions.

"Just like you saw Mytchel was married." Ta Meka reminded her. " Simone, sometimes we see what want to see." Ta Meka tried to point out to her cousin.

When Two Come Together

"I am going to go and talk to him when I get back to New York. I just couldn't do it that night," she told her cousins. "There no sense of calling because this not the type of thing you handle over the phone." The girls agreed. The rest of the flight they talked about the people from their old neighborhood. Once Simone reached Alabama, she decided that she would call Jonathan. First, she needed to check her e-mail and find. While she was reading there was a knock at the door. It was Mytchel clean and sober.

"Hey Simone" He kissed her on her cheek.

"Hey Mytchel," she welcomed him in. "How have you been?" She walked him over to her couch.

"I've been good. I stopped by because I need to talk to you," he answered. " I wanted to tell you that I know that I caused you a lot of pain and I understand that you and I could never be. I was just hoping that we could be friends." He looked for some type of response.

"Yea, I would like that" she smiled. "You know Graham had a stroke and I just got back in Alabama. However, you welcome to stay a while if you promise to excuse the mess," looking around the room.

"Nah, I have to go pick up Morgan, she going to spend the week with me." He kissed Simone on the cheek and was out the door. Simone watched Mytchel walk out of the door and realized that she was completely over him.

Aisha Johnson

    Simone went back to reading her e-mails, She had missed a lot at work. When she opened the last e-mail date Sat October 16th it hit her. Today was the 17th. Her period was a weak late. She grabbed her purse and headed down to corner drug store and to pick up a pregnancy test. *Damn* was all her mind could say. She went into her bathroom and the five minutes she waited for the results to show up, seemed like a couple of life times. *Oh my God two lines. I am Pregnant!*

When Two Come Together
Jonathan

Jonathan began to pack his clothes, he had to go to Philly for a few days and close a deal. When he was with Simone he was just going to commute. But since she was nowhere to be found he decided that maybe the best place for him was away from New York. It was 6:00 when he reached the hotel room. Jonathan decided that he would not sit around and feel pitiful about himself any longer. He decided to see what the city of "Brotherly Love" had to offer a brother. Jonathan decided to check out happy hour in the hotel restaurant. There were a lot of available seats but he chose to sit at the. Jonathan ordered a Long Island Ice-tea and a wings. He enjoyed his meal and watched the football game they had own. There were a few women there but no one who could make him forget about Simone. He went back to his room in sheer boredom. He called his house to check his messages and he was surprised to hear Simone's voice on the other end.

"Hey Jonathan, this is Simone. Can you please call me when you get a chance?" Jonathan didn't bother to listen to the rest of the messages. He called her from the hotel room.

"Hello," Simone picked up.

"Hey, this is Jonathan." Jonathan responded nervously.

"Oh I didn't recognized the number on the caller Id" Simone continued the conversation.

"I had to come to Philly to close that deal, remember?" He reminded her.

"Oh, yea." Simone recalled. " Jonathan I need to talk to you tonight and not over the phone." She got down to business.

"Well, I can drive back tonight it is no problem." Jonathan agreed.

"Or I can come there," She offered.

"You would do that?" He was shocked. She didn't answer. "You don't have to do that I am on my way."

Jonathan took a shower and headed back to New York. He was so happy that Simone had decided to just talk to him. It had been 3 weeks since had seen Simone's face. As he drove to her he thought about what he would say; how he would explain what she had seen? When he arrived at her place he could hear Simone's CD player. Before he knocked on the door he cut his cell phone off. He didn't need anyone interrupting this conversation.

When Two Come Together

Simone

Simone had spoken with Jonathan nearly and two hours ago. He said he was in Philly to work, but all Simone could think about, was that he was probably out the woman who she had seen kissing at the party. Simone had a lot of questions about that night. *Why did he even invite her if he knew she was going to be there? Why did he lie and say that he loved her when he didn't mean?* Simone decided now was not time to ask these questions. Things between her and Jonathan feel apart in seconds. Now that she was carrying his baby things were about to get even more complicated.

    Simone sipped her tea, and lost herself in the music. She wanted to tell the world that she was having a baby. She just didn't know how Jonathan was going to react and she need to know that first. When he knocked on the door she went to the mirror to be sure she had everything in tact and let him.

    "Hey" he smiled at her.

    "Hi," Simone looked up at him nervously "Come on in" It was weird not hugging him. Jonathan followed Simone to the couch and took a seat.

    "What you saw at the party-" Jonathan tried to explain. Simone cut him off.

    " Oh, I saw what I needed to see." Simone cut Jonathan off. "This isn't really about that" She explained. "I am pregnant with your baby" She continued.

    "For real?" he gleamed with joy.

    "Yea," Simone decided to see what he really thought. "I am getting an abortion" She lied.

    "No, no, no." Jonathan stood up. "Simone no." She could tell he was upset. Seeing the hurt in his eyes hurt her.

    Simone stood up to. " I have already decided. I don't want to have to do this alone"

When Two Come Together

"You won't, I swear." He kneeled down before and laid his ear against her stomach. He wrapped his arms around her waist and whispered.

"Simone, please don't kill our baby." Tears started to fall. They said nothing, but the room was not silent. Tears filled Simone eyes, as she heard the wails of a broken hearted man.

"Jonathan get up I am not going to kill our baby." I just need to know that you will be there for me and this baby." She said rubbing her stomach.

"Simone, I love you." He said, kissing her on her cheek. Simone walked to the kitchen and re-filled her cup of tea. She had decided that they should focuses on the baby only.

"This is not about us," she reminded Jonathan. They talked for hours. It was way to late for Jonathan to go anywhere so he slept on Simone's couch that night.

Aisha Johnson

Jonathan

Jonathan got up early. His trip to back to Philly was nice and quiet. It gave him time to clear his head. He couldn't believe that he was having a baby. He wanted to tell the world that he was going to be a father.

"Damn why did Tracey have to fuck my shit up?" he said athlete to himself. He wasn't mad at her, he just wanted to get things straight between him and Simone. He really didn't know the best way to approach the situation. He didn't know what to make of the relationship. The only thing he was sure of was that he going to be a great father.

Once Jonathan closed the deal he called his office to see if they could put another designer on the account and allow him to take a few days off.

When Two Come Together

On the way to Simone's house, he stopped at a local flower shop. He knew that flowers were not going to solve the entire problem, but it would be a start. Simone had not even allowed him to even tell her what was going on. She was so distracted by her hurt that she only wanted to focus on the baby. That was understandable. He just wanted to start dealing with the problem. Jonathan decided to stop by his place before going on over to Simone's. He wanted to check everything out, and get out of the business suit. He knew that Simone would probably be going to open mic night, if so he wanted to be prepared. It didn't matter what time he went to his apartment it always seemed so cold and lonely. Jonathan hated that feeling. He turned in the rental car, and caught a cab to Simone's place.

Aisha Johnson

Simone

When Simone woke up Jonathan was gone. He left a note saying that he would be back tonight. Simone loved Mondays because she got to open mic night. She started her walk to work a little early, because she wanted to call her grandmother and tell her the news about the baby. She smiled at the streets of New York realizing this was what she was here for, excitement. When she got there she had a client already waiting. She had forgotten all about the modeling agency. Simone got her Intern to go downstairs and open studio 4 since there were

When Two Come Together

twenty models they could assign two models to each dressing room.

"Mr. Alexander, I am Simone Benson" She extended her hand.

"Hello, Ms. Benson." He shook her hand," I am Todd Alexander."

The Agency had used the firm before but had complained about the professionalism of the staff. Mr. G put Simone in charge of the account because he felt that she would do a great job. Simone was excited about it because she rarely ever got the chance to go down to the studio's. The job was schedule to take atleast a month. She was putting together the photos that would be used on an international model search campaign

"I have these photos from a party we had for one of our models." He handed Simone the stack of pictures. He face froze when the top picture had Tonya and the girl she had seen kissing Jonathan. " If you could use those for anything please feel free to do so. You came highly recommended" He smiled.

"Thanks," Simone smiled. " What I would like to do is get group shots to day. Then meet with each individual model on separate appointments throughout the month. "

"That would be great" He smiled with approval. Simone called her intern into her office and gave her instructions on how to set up the appointments with each individual model. Then she headed down stairs for the photo shoot. Before going in she excused herself. She went into the restroom to check her hair and make up.

When Tonya spotted Simone she hurried over for quick conversation.

"Hey, How are you?"

"I am fine" Simone answered nervously and trying not to stare at Tracey. " How are you?"

"I am great. So what exactly do you do?" Tonya asked.

"I am a master photo editor, but I will be overseeing this entire account" she smiled. Tonya could see that Simone had her eyes fixed on Tracey. Once they completed the small talk she walked back over where the other models were and fixed the fly a ways on Tracey's hair. The day went by pretty fast. Simone couldn't believe she had to work under these conditions. When her intern brought her the paper she saw she had to supervise Tracey's shoot on Wednesday.

When Simone got home she decided that she would cook before open mic night, since Jonathan was coming over. She also decided that she was ready to talk, about what was going on between him and Tracey. She tried to figure out how to approach the subject, but it was 6:30, and Jonathan was at the door.

"Hey," he greeted her with flowers. As hard as she tried not to she couldn't help but smile. He

When Two Come Together

bent down and kissed her stomach. It felt so good to have him that close to her again.

"Hey, I am going to open mic night if you want, you can come." Simone invited yea

"Yea, as long as we can talk afterwards," Jonathan replied.

"Yea there are a lot of things I think that we need to sort out." Simone agreed. "Right now, let's eat.

Aisha Johnson

Jonathan

The food was delicious as always, Simone was a woman of many talents. Jonathan recognized that about her when they first started dating. The cab ride to open mic night was silent. Jonathan watched Simone gaze out of the window. *What is she thinking?* When they walked into Nikki's everyone was so glad that Simone was back. He wondered where she had been. She didn't even bother telling him that much. He wondered had she went back to her boyfriend, or just on vacation? Tonight he would have to get her to talk to him. When MC got on stage he recognized Simone's return and offered her the Mic first. She accepted.

"Hey Guys," She smiled and looked around into the crowed. "Thanks for missing me while I was away. I am back and I have something new to share with you."

Simone began to recite her poem.

When Two Come Together

Searching through the dimensions of my mind just
trying to find
peace of mind
I don't know who I am anymore.
He's trapped in every aspect of me.
damn my love for him lingers in my soul.
loved him so much I lost my identity
loved him so much I can't let go
I can't hate him
I can't have him
I don't know what to do
Believed him when everything he spoke was a lie
silly me
I allowed myself to be a victim
label me pitiful.
Too insecure to break free
His love was so destructive
Just too strong for me.
My heart is broken
Now I am incapable of loving again
wish he'd dissolve in my hurt
Break out my mind
all that would be left is memory
to bad that's not true
I wanna move on
I wanna grow
help me
God to let go
His voice spoke pleasure to my soul

Aisha Johnson

Thought once I had him I was whole
the truth be told
I was too weak
to be anything more that an extension of him
Unsure of how to be more than a friend
and less than everything.

Her eyes filled with tears, at the of the poem end she managed to squeeze out a thank you. Simone was ready go after that. She grabbed her purse and started walking out the door. Jonathan ran behind her. He was at a loss for words, so they walked in silence for the first couple of blocks in complete silence.

"Simone, I want to fix this" Jonathan started. "Can I at least explain to you what happen?" he asked.

"You were kissing a woman at a party that you invited me to. You embarrassed me, you disrespected me, and now I am carrying your baby." Simone began to speed up. "There is no way to fix this" Her tears were flowing.

"It wasn't really like that," Jonathan defended himself.

"Who is she to you?" Simone stopped walking and looked into Jonathan's eyes.

" She is my ex" Jonathan started.

When Two Come Together

"The ex, that wouldn't marry, your tired ass" Simone put her hand on her hips. "Whatever, Jonathan." Simone threw her hand up in his face.

"You think I would choose her over you?" He asked. "Simone, I am in love with you"

"Then why were you kissing her?" She questioned.

"I -I didn't kiss her, she kissed me." Jonathan attempted to explain. Simone began to walk again this time at faster pace. No words were being said, the Simone hailed a cab she saw coming down the block.

"Call me when you get ready to tell me the truth." Simone slammed the cab door in his face.

Jonathan walked home in deep thought. *Why did Simone have to be so damn dramatic?* She never wanted to listen to what really happen. She was always jumping to conclusions. He was tired of trying to open up the lines of communication with her. Maybe she didn't want them to work things out. She was everything she wanted, but maybe he wasn't enough. Maybe this was God's way of telling him that he deserved to be alone.

Simone

Aisha Johnson

Simone looked out on the city of New York, as she rode in the cab. New York had failed her once again. She was almost home when her cell phone rang. It was Mickey, the MC from Nikki's. He had gotten her number from Deborah. He wanted to talk to her and find out if everything was okay. He asked her if she wanted to join him for donuts and coffee. She agreed to meet him at a little coffee shop not to far from Nikki's. They talked about their poetry and his rap career. He was working on a demo, and hosting a few open mic nights around the city. He was a nice enough guy to talk to, and he was cute. Simone just wasn't trying to get involved with anyone. Jonathan had become a handful. They talked for a couple of hours and he walked her home. She told him all about Jonathan, and the baby. He told her how women, had tried to hold him down since he was trying to do his rap thing. He told her, his goals. Simone felt good about her new friend. It was just good to have someone to talk to. When Simone got to back to her apartment and went straight to bed. She could barely sleep thinking about being in the same room with Jonathan's whatever. So Simone pulled out her pen and began to write. As she wrote, she faded slowly into a deep sleep.

    The next morning, she woke up an hour earlier than normal. Simone decided that she wanted to look her best that meant she needed to

When Two Come Together

spiral curl her hair. Once she got dressed for work she decided to her grandmother.

"Hey Graham, how are you feeling?" Simone asked as cheerful as possible.

" Hey Simone, I am fine." Her grandmother answered. They went through the small talk. After stalling as long as she could, Simone delivered the news. "Graham I'm having a baby."

"When did you get married?" Her grandmother stated sarcastically. Simone couldn't believe that her grandmother was asking her that. She thought her grandmother would be excited. Simone took a deep breath and tried to calm herself.

"Graham, I'm not married, and at this point, I don't think I am ever getting married," Simone explained.

"You need to come home so that we can take care of that," her grandmother spoke firm and plainly.

"Take care of what?" Simone asked her grandmother with an *"I wish you would"* laugh.

"Your mistake" Her grandmother asked matter of fact. "You can't have a baby by a married man."

"First of all, this is not Mytch's baby" Simone's tone changed to hostile. " Secondly, I may not have planned for this baby, but it was not a mistake." Simone rubbed her belly. Thirdly, aren't you the same woman who told me that God doesn't make mistakes." Simone eyes filled with tears. This was not the response she had hoped for. The silence over the phone was short and bitter. "You know what Graham, Let me call you back." Simone didn't wait on a response she just hung up the phone.

Simone's anger prepared her for the meeting with Tracey Ellis. Simone tried to calm herself. She felt alone. She needed something or someone. She called the only rock she ever had.

"Mytchel," Simone said with emergency in her voice.

"Simone, Now is not a good time, can I call you back?" Mytchel said frustrated.

"You know what, Fuck you too." She said hanging up her the phone in his face. She walked down the busy streets of New York. The city she had once loved had now betrayed her. The city where the men were just as cold, if not colder, than the weather. She looked around and thought to herself this is the city that turned her grandmother against her. At this moment, she hated New York.

When Simone got to work, she was angry. She headed straight down to the studio to supervise Tracey's shoot. Simone could see why Jonathan was so attracted to her. She was beautiful. Her hair was just as long as Simone's. Her eyes were shaped like almonds. Her legs were long. It was as if God had created her to just to

When Two Come Together

be beautiful "Hello, I am Tracey Ellis." She said without a facial expression.

Simone forced a smile on her face. " I am Simone Benson." They shook hands firmly. Simone studied her beauty as the photographer snapped the pictures. She couldn't help but think *this woman better not cross me.* Simone wondered if the tension obvious to other people around them..

The shoot was nice and quiet as both women tried to stay out of each other's way. Once the shoot was over that said their brief good-byes and Simone headed back to her office.

"Excuse me," Tracey uttered trying to catch up to her. "Would you mind if I could talk to you for a second?"

All Simone could think was *hell yea I mind.* "Come and follow me to my office." Simone closed the door and tried to prepare herself for what this woman was about to say. Simone was nervous. She had already loss her man to Tracey, she prayed for God to keep her calm. She didn't want to loose her job too. Simone offered her seat and sat down behind her desk.

"I know that you know who I am," Tracey said with no emotion.

"Excuse me," Simone tried to maintain her professionalism.

"I am Jonathan's ex-fiancé," Tracey began to peak " I wanted to apologize to you personally for the night of the party." Tracey began. " It is just that me and John have a real history together. I never imagine that when we broke up last year that it was really over."

Simone couldn't believe what she was hearing. She remained silent so that she could take it all in.

"You are really lucky to have a man like him, and I hope that you will take good care of him" Tracey got up to leave. Before she could get to the door, Simone stopped her.

"Thanks," she smiled at Tracey.

Simone still wasn't sure of exactly what was going on. She sat in silence for a monument to figure things. She pulled out Mickey's number to get his advice. Just as she was about to dial the number, she hung up the phone. Simone got her purse and headed for the door.

Jonathan

Jonathan sat in his living room playing his X-box. This was one of the very few things he did that kept his mind off of Simone and the baby. Jonathan, still hadn't told anyone about the baby. He was very excited, he just wasn't ready for all the drama that surrounded the news. He wanted to tell his parents, but the he still wasn't sure that Simone wasn't going to get that abortion. If Simone decided to keep the baby, he would be the first of his friends to have a baby. Jonathan was so enthralled in the basketball game, that the door shocked him. He looked through the peep-hole and it was Simone. Jonathan opened the door.

"Hey" she nervously. " Sorry, I didn't call. Do you have a minute?" She asked looking down.

"Yea, sure" Jonathan stepped aside and let Simone walk in. "Can I get you something to drink?"

" Nah," She paused "I'm cool." Simone walked over to Jonathan's couch. " I wanted to apologize to you."

" For what?" Jonathan questioned.

"For not talking, not listening, not fighting, not thinking, not trusting that I love you." Simone said with tears in her eyes.

"What brought this on?" asked while sitting down next to her.

Simone looked him in his eyes and whispered softly, "I love you."

"I love you too!" Jonathan said as he moved in for a kiss.

The two sat in Jonathan's apartment and began to talk about there relationship where it was and where it was going. When Simone left Jonathan he called his parent and delivered the news about the baby. Then he called Mark and Tony, and told them. Before the night was over he had called every body he knew, then headed over to Simone's place.

Simone

Simone looked at her watch, she had been dreading this call. She picked up the phone, and called her grandmother.

"Hey Graham," Simone tried to sound excited.

"Hey baby. How are you feeling?" Her grandmother asked with concern in her voice.

"I am good," Simone answered.

"So when am I going to meet the new fellow, who got you breaking all of God's laws?" Her grandmother questioned her.

"Soon" She smiled at just the thought of Jonathan.

"Graham, I hope that you can understand that this is happy time for us." Simone explained.

"Simone, I am happy too. I just want to make sure that you aren't short changed. I have always wanted the best for you.

"I am sorry, that I let you down." Simone lowered her tone of voice.

"You haven't let me down, you made a great grandmother, If you are happy then so am I" her grandmother re-assured her. The women talked for a little longer and the Graham had to go.

The rain drew Simone to the window, she stood watching and listening to the rain. This was New York City, the city that she loved more then any other city in the world. This was the city that loved her back. The city that gave her wings and taught her to fly. The city that only did things to make her stronger. She smiled, she was finally happy.

When Two Come Together

Excerpt:
His Infidelities

Aisha Johnson

    Mia looked at her watch. David's flight should be landing any minute now. She giggled to her self. After 6 years of marriage, she still got excited every time her husband came home from seminars, conferences, or workshops. Sometimes Mia felt guilty for not being able to travel with her husband. It was just that her job as director of the community center wouldn't allow it. She could tell that David really missed her. Whenever he returned from one of his trips, they would always make love something serious, no matter what time his plane landed. David would send her to the heavens and back during sex. Mia was enthralled by thoughts of what her husband had in store for her. She was shocked when David walked up behind her and kissed her on the curve of her neck.

    "Miss Me? " She asked as she smiled and turned towards him.

    "You know I did, baby. He answered grabbing her hand pulling her closer to him. They walked out to the car hand in hand talking about his trip and everything that went on while he was away. Mia looked at her watch. It was 4:30. Maybe after sex she could get an evening run in. Things at the center had been hard lately because she was trying to help clear up some of the problems that the kids were having that were centered around racism. Mia decided that she wasn't even going to start thinking about that. Her man was home, and it had been three long nights.

When Two Come Together

As they traveled down the freeway, Mia decided to get an early start on pleasing David. She placed her hand onto his lap and slid it up his thigh. She slowly unbuckled his belt. Mia watched as a smile magically appeared across David's face. She pulled out his penis and rubbed it slowly. Mia leaned over and ran her tongue down his manhood. His cell phone rang and he glanced at the caller id. He motioned for Mia to stop, but he could tell that she was aggravated. The call lasted the whole way home. Mia assumed that it was just one of his patients because he kept telling the person on the other end that.

"You don't have to do it alone. I am here for you." The first thing David did when he got home was to take a shower. By the time Mia brought his dinner and all of his mail up to him, David was snoring like a baby. Mia's feelings were hurt. As long as David had been working a Donald and Harrison, as many trips as he had taken, he had never come home and just went to sleep.

Mia decided not to sweat it. She changed into her running clothes and went for an evening run. That was what she liked most about the summer. Every once in a while she got a chance to enjoy the evening wind. Today, she had at least 2 hours of good sunlight left after doing everything she needed to do. With each stride, Mia released a little of the stress she was carrying from her job. Running always allowed her to clear her head.

Four miles Mia said to herself as she hit her doorstep. Before she could get into her door, Mr. Marks called her over.

"Hi there Mia," Mr. Marks smiled. He motioned for her to come to his yard.

"Hi," she smiled puzzled by his invite to come over. They had been living in Carrington Falls for years, and she couldn't ever recall a time when he had invited her over before.

"How are you?"

"I am great." He smiled harder. " I wasn't sure if David was home or not, so I thought I would just check on you." He said casually. Mia tried not to look too confused, but as long as they had been living there, Mr. Marks had never seemed to care about Mia's well being before.

"Thanks for asking Mr. Marks, but I am fine." Mia smiled.

"David is home."

"You can call me Alex," he said. "I'm just worried because he is gone so much, and well, I saw some teenage thugs coming through like they were checking out the place." The two chatted for a second longer, and Mia headed inside for a shower. Mia couldn't help but think about what Alex had said. Carrington Falls was an upscale area, and there was a very low crime rate. David was still sleeping when she climbed into bed with him. Mia was bored, and it was still early, so she decided to wake David.

When Two Come Together

"Unh," He answered. He was still too sleepy to open his eyes.

"Baby, I am bored. We should be doing something," Mia said frustrated. "Dancing or Dessert," she continued.

David lifted his head off the pillow and smiled at Mia. "Desert sounds great!" He said excited. "Bring me something back," he mumbled as he dove his head back into the pillow. Mia went down stairs and pulled out the Vanilla Ice-cream. She fixed herself a big bowl and added whipped cream and strawberries, then, headed to the den. She watched HBO until she fell asleep. Mia woke up and made her way to the bedroom. It was 3:30 in the morning.

"Where have you been?" David asked softly and concerned.

"In the den," Mia answered climbing into the bed.

"I'm sorry I fell asleep," David said in almost a whisper.

"It's alright," Mia lied.

She was upset because David didn't make love to her. The next morning they moved around the house in silence. Mia noticed that David hadn't even kissed her good-bye this morning. Once she got to work, she found it hard to concentrate on her paperwork. Mia needed to see what was up with her husband. She decided to take an early lunch and visit his job.

Aisha Johnson

The traffic was heavy on the freeway during lunchtime. There were at least three accidents and a stray dog on the freeway. Mia hated coming into the city because it seemed like pure chaos most of the time. She reserved coming into the city for Lakers games and Christmas parties. When Mia reached her husband's firm, she made a pit stop in the ladies room. She hadn't been to his office in nearly a year, and she wanted to be sure that she was together.

As Mia turned the corner where her husband's office was located, she saw him talking to a pregnant woman. She added a little pep in her step because she loved to meet her husband's clients whenever she got a chance. As she got closer, she saw David rub his hand over the pregnant woman's belly and then kiss her. Anger filled her as she screamed his name.

"Mia," David answered in shock.

"Who is this?" Mia asked pointing to the woman. She got no answer. The elevator buzzed, and the lady was about to step on. Mia instructed her not move.

"Go ahead," David said over Mia.

"Who are you?" Mia asked the lady, but she got no answer. "Who is this bitch?" Mia asked again. " Why were you kissing my husband?" She questioned the lady. "Do you know that he has been married for 6 long years?" Mia dropped her purse to the floor and looked at David. "I can't believe you." Tears began to flood her eyes and her head began to spin. "Whose baby is it?" Mia got no answer from David. She got no tears, no explanation, no apologies.

"Is that my husband's baby?" Mia asked the lady.

"If it is?" the woman snapped back at Mia.

"Do I look like a fucking toy to you?" Mia jumped into the woman's face. "Here you are fucking my husband, and you want to play with me?" Mia lost control and grabbed the woman.

"Mia!" David grabbed her. "Can you please calm down?" He begged. "We can discuss this when I get home."

"Calm down? Calm down? Hell no, I will not calm down!" Mia picked her purse up from the floor.

"Get a way from my husband!" She pushed the lady a few steps back. "Stay away from my damn husband." Mia grabbed David's hand and flashed his wedding band. Mia stood with her hands on her hips as she watched the lady get on the elevator and go down to the first floor. "I can't believe you," Mia said coldly as she walked backwards towards the steps.

The ride home seemed much shorter than normal. That may have been due to the fact that she did 110 constantly, only stopping for red lights and stop signs. Mia called the center and told them she wouldn't be back in, and to have all calls transferred to her voicemail.

The moment she stepped into her house, she kicked off her shoes and went up stairs. She pulled her loc's back into a ponytail and changed out of her work clothes. She went out to the garage and pulled out a few moving boxes. Mia wasted no time heading to her bedroom. She labeled the first box *T-shirts, boxers, ties and socks.* The second box was labeled *Pants (slacks, jeans, and etc).* Mia realized what she was doing and started to just throw his things in a box. She called David on his cell phone and got no answer. " Of course your sorry ass wouldn't answer the phone. It is now 3:26. If you don't come and got your shit by 6:00, I am going to pull a *waiting to exhale* on your ass." Mia slammed the phone down and fixed herself a glass of red wine.

She laid across the couch thinking of her next move. Should she call his momma first or hers? Should she call her brother or sister? Should she call his sister? What had she done to deserve this? Mia allowed questions and insecurities rock her to sleep. It was 5:47 when David walked in. " Leave your key on the night stand by my bed," Mia said with an attitude.

David walked over to the couch and stood over her.

"So you don't want to talk about this?" he asked.

When Two Come Together

"What is there to talk about? You stuck your dick in another woman, broke our vows, and now you have a baby on the way. That seems to be the gist of it." Mia sat up and waited on David's response. She got nothing.

"When were you going to tell me?" Mia's voice cracked with pain.

"I just found out that she was pregnant," David screamed in his defense.

"You knew you fucked her, you could have told me that." Mia reminded him of his infidelity. "Where did you meet her? Why did you cheat? Mia stood up from the couch. Didn't I cook? Didn't I clean? I washed your dirty under wear. I made the bed. I help pay the bills. Hell, I even swallowed. What else could I have done to make this fucking marriage work?" Tears began to stream down her face.

"Mia, you know that me cheating had nothing to do with you."

"Everything you do directly affects me, that's is why it's called marriage." Mia lifted his hand to remind him of the ring. " What about our vows and our plans David?"

"Baby, I'm sorry. David kneeled before Mia. "If you give me a chance, we can talk about this, fix this, you know *for better or worse,*" David pleaded. He grabbed Mia from her waist and pulled her close to him and whispered in her ear, "I love you." A weird silence filled the room as they stood face to face, no tears, no answers, just hurt. David broke the silence. "Please don't turn me away."

Mia pulled back. She looked over her husband. This was the man of her dreams, the only man she ever loved. David was the first man she ever really respected. He was the only man who had been inside of her. The only man that made her moan. The man whose freckles she had played connect the dots with. This was her husband. She ran her fingers hair through his dark, thick, curls and then all over his well defined face. She rubbed her hands across his nearly perfect chest. She sniffed his cologne. This looks like her husband, felt like her husband, smelled like her husband, but this couldn't be her husband. The David Dawson Jr. that she married would have never hurt her.

"I'm not sure if I want you to go or stay." Mia spoke honestly. "I don't know what to do." She sat down on the couch and made room for him. He sat on the floor so that they could be face to face.

"Let's work it out, go to counseling, or do whatever it takes." David pleaded.

Mia's head began to spin. She couldn't make a decision like that this soon. There was a baby involved. "Is it a boy or a girl?" Mia asked

"I don't know," David answered.

"David, why don't you know? It *is* your baby." Mia waited for confirmation.

When Two Come Together

"Mia, I hadn't seen or talked to Lisa since I ended it with her. It lasted for 4 days, and I told her that I was in love with my wife. She called on yesterday and told me that she was having the baby any day now."

"Any day now?" Mia repeated what he had said to be sure that she understood what he saying.

"Yes. I would have told you about the affair and the baby way before now. I would have owned up to my sins. I just thought all of that was behind me." David admitted.

"So, how sure are we that the baby is yours?" Mia questioned.

"She said that she had not been with anyone else, and she is the kind of-" David attempted to defend what was left of Lisa's honor.

"Of what?" Mia interrupted. "She slept with a married man. *She is that kind of woman.*" Mia pointed out the hard truth. "Why did she wait so long to call you?" Mia asked.

"She said that she understood that I had decided to stay with you. She said she didn't want to ruin our marriage."

"David, that is bullshit, and you know it." Mia screamed. "It is way too late for all that. She should have thought about that before she fucked you the first time. Why didn't the bitch have an abortion?"

"She said she would have but really couldn't force herself to take a life." David tried to show Mia a different side to things.

"What is the difference? She fucked up my life and damn near had you killed."

"What?" David looked confused.

"Yes, the thought of killing you crossed my mind several times today." Mia cracked a smile, but she wasn't joking. "So, she might as well have killed the little fucker, anyway."

"Mia!" David grabbed her. "Calm down, I don't want you to say anything negative about the baby. Do you understand?" His eyes were filled with anger. She could tell that her comments had hurt David. Mia smiled on the inside. She wanted him to feel some pain.

"David, all I meant to say was, I am not buying her bullshit. The baby may not even be yours." Mia cleaned up her previous statement. She looked over at her husband and notice that the anger had left his eyes and it looked more like hurt. She walked over to him and rubbed his arm. "What is the matter?"

When Two Come Together

Aisha Johnson
Discussion Questions

1. Have you ever been involved with a married man and didn't know it? Did you react the way Simone did?

2. Do you think that Simone and Jonathan waited to long to have sex? How long is two long?

3. Do you think Simone over reacted to the kiss she saw between Tracey and Jonathan? Why?

4. Do you think that Tracey made the right decision by choosing her modeling career over Jonathan? Why? What would you have done?

5. Why do think Jonathan slept with Tracey again?

6. Do you think that Simone should have moved back home to take care of grandmother?
Why or Why not? (Remember her grandmother raised her after her parents died.)

7. How do you feel about Simone's grandmother reaction to the news she was pregnant?

8. How do you feel about Simone and Jonathan's relationship now? Do you think they will be together forever now?

When Two Come Together

Order Form

Name:			
Address:			
City		State	Zip

Title	Qty	Price
Secret Blessing		16.95
I Am		12.95
When Will My Birds Sing?		14.95
When Two Come Together		12.95
Wait For Love: A Black Girl's Story		16.95
"No More Faking It (Sister's Talk Candidly About Sex)		14.95
"Love Don't Live Here...It Just Visits		12.95

        Subtotal
        S&H ($2.00 per book) _____
        Total Enclosed _____

Send check/money order to:
Nubiangodess Publishing
PO Box 12224
Columbus, Georgia 31917-2224

Make check/money order payable to: Angela Weathered
Book clubs: If you order 10 or more copies, you receive a 10% discount.

Aisha Johnson

When Two Come Together

Aisha Johnson

When Two Come Together

Aisha Johnson